OPERATION COBALT

LL RICHMAN

CONTENTS

ABOUT THE BIOGENESIS WAR UNIVERSE

Humanity has reached the stars.

With colonies established throughout the Sol System, explorers hungry for new ventures traveled beyond its borders to colonize nearby Alpha Centauri.

At the same time, a brave pair of ships set their sights a bit farther afield—on the binary stars Procyon and Sirius. Those who settled there called themselves the Geminate Alliance.

Such distances made interaction prohibitive. Even with the Scharnhorst drive's ability to triple the speed of light, travel between the colonies was measured in months, if not years.

In the mid-twenty-fifth century, that all changed. The Geminate Alliance stunned the known worlds with the invention of the Calabi-Yau Gate. The gates folded space, enabling instantaneous travel between star systems. True interstellar commerce became a reality.

The Alliance as a whole prospered, but like in any nation, there were pockets of discontent. Free speech allowed dissenters a voice, but some weren't content with that platform.

In a less-populated sector of Sirian space, one such group decided to do something about it....

"Victorious warriors win first and then go to war, while defeated warriors go to war first and then seek to win."
~ Sun Tzu

"The way to win in a battle … is to know the rhythms of the specific opponents, and use rhythms that your opponents do not expect."
~ Miyamoto Musashi, *The Book of Five Rings*

ONE

CMS *GOBLIN*
COBALT MINING SECTOR TWELVE
BIG BLUE (SIRIUS A)

"FRED, NO! THAT'S not a chew toy!"

Katie Hyer planted her boots against the hatch she'd just sealed and pushed away from the surface. The action sent her shooting across the cramped space toward the mining tug's cockpit.

The strains of a catchy, old-Earth tune filtered from the ship's audio system as she snagged the pilot's seat with one hand to arrest her forward motion. A reluctant smile tugged at her lips when she heard Carrie Underwood's voice belt out something about the more men she's around, the more she loves her hound.

Jeremy's timing, as usual, was impeccable. The traffic controller who worked Cobalt Mining's first shift liked to spin the tunes during times when there weren't any ships coming or going from the Sierra Twelve platform. Tuesdays were what he called 'country music day'—whatever that meant. Katie had yet to figure out which country the music represented.

"Betcha Underwood's dog never tried eating his own safety net," she muttered as she reached for her pet.

The dog was floating butt-first just above the co-pilot's seat, net clamped firmly between his jaws. The remainder waved in the null-g environment as he yanked the material back and forth.

She reached for a corner when it floated her way, but Fred intuited her intent. The basset puppy kicked against the copilot's chair and went flying toward the back of the ship. Katie sighed and followed.

The netting wasn't hers; it belonged to Cobalt Mining. She'd intended to return it to the dock earlier in the week, but Fred's baby seat hadn't yet arrived, so she needed it to keep him secure when she was maneuvering the ship.

Fred thought this was a fun, new game; she could see it in his eyes. His floppy ears haloed around him as he sailed across the small cabin. They flattened against the aft bulkhead when he bumped against it with a muffled *oof*.

Or was that a woof? she wondered.

She caught up to him and tugged at the drool-slicked material clamped between his jaws. Fred doubled down, emitting a cute baby growl.

"No!" she scolded. "You can't eat your seat belt. Now, gimme!"

He let out another growl as a great gob of slobber went floating through the cabin.

Katie sighed once more, and called out to the ship's Synthetic Intelligence. "*Goblin*, release containment nano, please. Cabin bulkhead, aft."

From the corner of her eye, Katie caught a flicker of light as a haze of glittering specks leached from the bulkhead to envelop the floating droplets. A slight breeze grazed her cheek, and she knew the ship was directing the airflow to recall the nano back into the fabric of the bulkhead.

She eyed her recalcitrant pet. "Well, at least you left your diaper alone this time."

Intellectually, she knew that *Goblin*'s containment nano could just as easily herd any errant puppy pee into the ActiveFiber coating that layered the ship's bulkheads, but the thought kind of grossed her out.

Katie gave the cargo netting another sharp tug, her feet planted against the aft bulkhead. Fred let go and Katie went rocketing back the way she'd come, her head rapping sharply against the bulkhead separating the cockpit from the tiny cabin.

With a small groan, she dragged her hand through her shock of maroon curls, fingers poking at the tender spot the medical nano in her body was already in the process of healing.

Schooling her face into stern lines, she shook the liberated material at him in mock-threat.

"Bad boy, Fred! Bad! This is *not* a toy!"

Fred looked back at her with large, sad, brown eyes. She relented, gathering him up in her arms and placing a kiss on his forehead.

Her attention snapped back to the ship when the music cut out and *Goblin*'s SI announced, *{Warning! Unknown vessel approaching! Intercept heading!}*

Katie's training kicked in. "Show me that ship," she ordered, shoving Fred into the co-pilot's chair and securing him with quick, practiced motions.

The view on *Goblin*'s main holoscreen shifted to show the incoming vessel. With a muttered curse, Katie slammed herself into her own seat.

Fingers flew over the pilot's board as she brought the drives online and sent the tug into a steep dive. Far from the nimble response she would have liked, the ship turned exactly as expected: like a bloated whale.

She saw instantly that *Goblin* lacked the control authority to evade. It couldn't, not with the load of metal ores tied to its back end. With a twinge of regret, she triggered the quick-release and the tow hook assembly floated free.

She tried again. This time, freed from its encumbrance, the tug leapt forward like a thoroughbred released from the starting gate, *Goblin*'s massive fusion drives dodging the approaching vessel with ease.

Katie switched the forward viewscreen to the aft sensor feed, mentally bracing for a collision between the newcomer and the asteroid chunks she'd just ejected—but it never came. The ship, still flying dark, jinked out of the way, thrusters firing in a complex dance.

Katie was reluctantly impressed. Whoever was handling that vessel knew what they were doing.

She let out an annoyed grunt when the ship's thrusters bestowed a spin to the netted ores—a spin she'd now have to match in order to reacquire her load.

With one last twitch, the ship raced away, on a course that led right to Sierra Twelve.

"Jerks. Ever heard of karma?" Katie addressed the departing spacecraft. "Hope yours ends up biting you in the ass."

TWO

DAP Helios, GNS Scimitar
Decommissioned mining platform
0.9 Astronomical Units from Sierra Twelve

Twenty-eight hours earlier....

THE MYSTERIOUS SHIP that had nearly sideswiped *Goblin* was flying dark for a reason. Its frantic pace was the result of a run-in with an Alliance Navy vessel.

GNS *Scimitar* was a fast-action Helios, the stealthed version of one of the most ubiquitous utility ships in the Geminate Navy. Though the Helios was a familiar enough sight in the Alliance military, one look at *Scimitar*'s unique profile and adaptive coatings was enough to make any criminal turn tail and run.

Scimitar's flight crew should have been on their way home after having retrieved a Tier One team from an operation deep within the Sirius system—but just as Rafe, the ship's pilot, set course for the star's heliopause, an invitation arrived.

Micah Case, *Scimitar*'s co-pilot, was the first to see the incoming message. He lifted a brow as he read its contents, silently passing it on to Rafe. Rafe, in turn, sent it on to Team Five, the Special Recon unit that now occupied *Scimitar*'s aft cabin.

The invitation was simply worded:

> From: James Bridgetree, Commander, 76th Coast Guard Regiment.
> To: Lane Reid, Captain, SRU Team Five.
> The 76th invites you to an impromptu war game...

The message then spat out a string of coordinates.

No words needed to be said; Micah and Rafe were both certain it would be turned down. To the surprise of both men, Reid accepted. The two men exchanged a bemused look, and then both set themselves to the task of turning the ship around.

{Flip and burn in five seconds,} Rafe announced over the shipnet.

{What the hell, Cap?} The voice of Dana, the crew's gunner broke in on the flight crew's private channel. *{The gate's in the other direction.}*

A quick glance over at Rafe told Micah the pilot was engaged in conversation with someone—Reid, most likely.

{Looks like Reid's team is going to play war games with the coast guard,} Micah supplied.

{Coasties?} Cass DeWitt echoed from her flight engineer's position behind Rafe.

{Sounds like,} Micah agreed.

{Huh. War games?} asked Dana.

{That's what the message that came in said,} he told her. *{It was in the clear, so I'm taking it at face value.}*

{Huh,} she repeated.

Micah couldn't tell if Dana's *huh* meant she was surprised that Team Five would accept, or that she expected the coasties to be handed their asses in short order.

Probably both.

Additional telemetry came in from the 76th, directing them to their rendezvous. While Rafe set *Scimitar* on that heading, Micah deployed the sphere of surveillance and reconnaissance drones that were his responsibility as co-pilot. Not that the maps indicated anything other than micrometeorite dust between here and there, but a Shadow Recon pilot left nothing to chance.

A few hours later, the crew found themselves closing on an abandoned mining platform in the middle of the black. As Rafe brought the Helios in on a smooth arc, Micah considered just how asymmetrical a mock skirmish would be between the 76th and the special forces operators seated in the back of the ship. Over the flight crew's private comm channel, he voiced his thoughts to Rafe.

{Turns out the 76th's garrison commander is an old friend of Reid's and heard through the grapevine they were in the area,} Rafe replied. *{Apparently, she owes him one and he just called in the favor. Guess he feels his coasties need to be shaken up a bit.}*

Dana's sarcastic *{Ya think?}* brought a grin to Micah's face. Then a warning chime sounded, and he gave the approaching platform his full attention.

According to the automated signal of a stationary buoy floating a hundred thousand klicks spinward, the mining platform belonged to the Cobalt Mining Consortium. The buoy's broadcast informed any comers that the platform was now closed.

A follow-up transmission from the 76th filled in the rest: the mining platform had reached the end of its useful life, and so Cobalt had it decommissioned six months ago. It was scheduled for demolition in the coming year, but in the interim, the coast guard had gained Cobalt's permission to conduct exercises aboard the abandoned structure.

Scimitar approached from stellar north, and as they neared, Rafe dropped an icon onto an access hatch.

{That's where the team will insert.}

Micah nodded. *{Copy that.}*

{Keep monitoring nearspace, in case the coasties decide to get clever and sneak a second wave of sailors aboard, to flank Reid's team,} Rafe added.

{That'd liven things up,} said Dana.

Cass snorted. *{Yeah, it'd take 'em a good ten minutes longer to ferret them out.}*

{Cass,} Rafe called warningly, and the flight engineer responded by giving his pilot's seat a shove with her booted foot

{Fine. I'll behave.}

None of *Scimitar's* crew had any doubts about the outcome of today's exercise, though Cass and Dana had begun placing bets on how long it would take the Unit men and women to sort the coasties and call for an extraction.

Micah tuned them out, opting to listen in on the team's combat channel as they geared up instead.

His lips twitched when he heard, *{**Paintballs**? Are you fucking kidding me, hoss?}*

The voice belonged to Thad Severance, Team Five's second-in-command. A hulking Marine with dark skin and an easy smile, the man had the mind of a brilliant tactician and could give intimidation lessons to an apex predator.

Micah's smile widened as Thad continued to rant, his tone dripping with disgust. Clearly, he thought a paintball gun was a wuss thing for a Marine to carry.

{Dude. These are coasties,} came an exasperated reply. *{You can't play with your usual toys, capiche? Plus, I spiked it with a little something extra.}* That was Jack Campbell, the team's intel officer and hacker extraordinaire.

He was also a licensed pilot, the only one on Team Five. That skill come in handy more than once in recent years. When the team couldn't make it to the prearranged extraction point, Jack had commandeered whatever local skiff he could get his hands on, while the flight crew aboard *Scimitar* reconfigured, navigating to the fallback site instead.

Apparently, Jack had just added to his skill set, branching out into weapons design by modifying a child's toy into an offensive weapon.

Through the ship's aft feed, Micah saw Thad pick up the plastic-handled weapon to examine it more closely. His hands dwarfed the thing.

{You spiked it,} the big Marine repeated. *{You mean you integrated a Spike into the paintball itself?}*

{Yep.} Jack sounded smug. *{Tag one of 'em and they're going to be wearing more than a bright blue spot. With the Spike's electronic breadcrumb trail, you'll be able to track them anywhere they go.}*

{That's an unfair advantage, Lieutenant.} Lane Reid looked up from where she'd been cleaning her knife to level a hard look at Jack.

{Aw, c'mon, Cap, **we're** *an unfair advantage,}* he protested. *{Besides, it gives us a chance to test out a new piece of gear in a semi real-world application, with none of the risk. How often do we get that?}*

*{You can't be serious. You plan to add blue **paintballs** to our arsenal?}* Elodie Cyr pulled to a stop in front of the intelligence officer, one hand wrapped around her sniper's rifle. The other held a blue ball between thumb and finger as if it were a deadly contagion. She looked as incredulous as she sounded.

{This is just a prototype,} Jack assured her. *{And no, the end product won't be embedded in a ball of blue paint.}*

Ell grunted and palmed the ball as she turned away, but otherwise refused to respond.

Undaunted, Jack continued handing out his modified paintball guns. They joined the team's standard loadout of carbyne blades, flash-bang grenades, pulse pistols, and flechettes.

By the time they were done, *Scimitar* had come to rest alongside the maintenance hatch. Rafe deployed the umbilical; from that point, it took the team less than five minutes to enter the platform and seal the hatch behind them.

As Rafe focused on the delicate dance of holding station a scant few meters from the platform's skin, Micah returned his attention to the sphere of drones that encased the Helios in a protective sphere.

With the exception of the two teams playing an elaborate game of capture-the-flag, and a decent-sized coast guard cutter on the platform's opposing side, the area *should* have been abandoned.

And it was… for about half an hour.

The flight crew kept an open channel with *Scimitar*'s end muted, while Reid met with Bridgetree and they hammered out the rules of engagement and then dispersed. Twenty minutes later, the teams' HUDs flashed green and the hunt was on.

Micah's attention was split between the team's feed and the constellation of drones deployed in nearspace, around the section of mining platform where *Scimitar* hovered. Fifteen minutes into the exercise, a blip caught Micah's eye.

He waited for it to repeat, and when it didn't, he sent a quick mental command to the swarm of drones he controlled. The tiny vessels turned in a tight curve, angling back toward the EM signature that had disappeared just as quickly as it had shown up. Moments later, he had a visual.

{Contact!} he sang out, sending the feed to Cass to verify. *{Two ships, just cresting the top of the platform.}*

{Are they coasties?} asked Rafe.

{Checking,} Cass replied. Then, a beat later, *{Nope, the cutter says they're not.}*

Dana interrupted, her voice taut. *{Hey, Cap? Their signature indicates they're weapons hot.}*

That caused Micah to straighten. He'd been sure the ships were part of the 76th's assault plan.

The initial blip morphed into a more detailed visual of the approaching vessels as Micah's drones filled in the missing information. He sent it to *Scimitar*'s forward holoscreens.

That drew a grunt of displeasure from the man seated to Micah's right. Rafe's hands danced over his controls, and in the next instant, the slightest tremor shuddered through the ship.

An alert accompanied the action, appearing on Micah's overlay. It informed him Rafe had just jettisoned the umbilical that tethered them to the platform's hatch. A second telltale followed the first, this one indicating the airlock had just cycled shut.

Scimitar was on the move.

{Noble One, this is Spartan.} Rafe's voice cut in over Team Five's

combat net. *{We have two unidentified ships, armed and assumed hostile. I say again, armed ships, assumed hostile. Breaking away to engage.}*

Rafe's brief comm was met with silence, but that didn't worry Micah overmuch. If the hostiles' presence extended to the platform, it was possible they'd made contact and were already engaging.

Micah almost felt sorry for their surprise guests. If there was criminal intent, no team was better equipped to take them out than SRU Team Five.

The Helios drifted silently away, Rafe's deft hand at the controls seamlessly reconfiguring the ship's tunable outer layer from a reflectance that matched the platform to one that emulated the blackness of space.

Scimitar was now effectively a ghost, with full stray-light suppression on all EM bands. The chances of the two unmarked hostiles finding the Shadow Recon ship were next to none, but that didn't mean its flight crew were going to sit on their hands while a threat lurked nearby.

* * *

Thad had taken a knee and was looking at a pile of rubble through the reticle of his P-SCAR rifle, debating whether he was looking at a trap set by the coasties, when the call from *Scimitar* came through.

{Noble Two, this is Spartan. Do you copy?}

Thad did a slow visual sweep of the area. He sent a brief, two-click acknowledgment as he slid back toward the concealment provided by the passageway.

{Unable to reach Noble One,} the voice continued. *{We have a situation.}*

Rafe's update was delivered in the preternaturally calm voice all Shadow Recon pilots seemed to have, no matter how tense things got. As he listened, Thad turned the news over in his tactician's mind.

{You sure they're not coasties?}

{They don't fit the profi—} Thad heard Micah swear as he abruptly cut off, only to come back in the next instant with an update. *{Negative, Tango One is now closing on the coastie ship.}*

Thad scrubbed the stubble on the side of his face. *Well, ain't that just a fine kettle of fish.*

He turned and motioned the two team members on his six to come forward. When they were within range, he reached out to establish an untraceable, peer-to-peer connection.

{We have a new player, not connected to the 76th. Assume active hostiles.}

The woman facing him remained impassive, but the demolitions man crouching beside her lifted a brow, and his gaze slid sideways. *{And here you thought this exercise would be boring, Sarge.}*

He elbowed the sniper lightly—or would have, had Ell's hand not whipped out and twisted the man's arm behind his back.

{Ow, dammit!}

{You were saying, sir?}

Thad buried a smile as he glanced back toward the intersection.

{We need to make contact with the coasties. Let them know we have company, and the exercise is off.}

Ell released Mike's arm and then shot Thad a considering look. *{I can climb overhead, drop behind them and deliver the message.}*

Thad nodded. *{Go.}*

She slung her P-SCAR rifle over her shoulder, crossed on light feet to the bulkhead, and then began her silent ascent. Spars ridged the bulkhead's surface in regular intervals, making it easy for the sniper to find purchase. The sticky organogel threads lining the palms of her drakeskin suit would enable her to remain there indefinitely.

Halfway up the wall, Ell engaged her suit's active stealth and faded from sight. Thad's suit kept track of her, its predictive systems using the team's connection to track her telemetry, her position showing as a ghostly outline over his HUD.

That part of his plan in place, Thad glanced over at Mike. *{Rafe couldn't raise the captain. Find her and give her a sitrep.}*

He brought up a schematic of the platform, and dropped a pin on its control center *{We know she was headed here. If she's not responding, chances are that she, Jack, and Asha have already had a run-in with whoever's out there badgering* Scimitar. *Round up any coasties you find along the way.}*

Mike nodded. *{Yessir.}*

Thad squinted at the pile of rubble. *{Stay frosty and don't get yourself caught. In the meantime, I think I'll do a little tracking myself.}*

{Good hunting, LT.} The demolitions man rose and crept silently down the passageway, the platform's emergency lighting lending an eerie cast to his form before he faded from view.

* * *

Rafe had brought *Scimitar* around on the same heading as the ship bearing down on the coast guard cutter, kicking thrusters to maximum in order to gain on the unmarked vessel.

{ECM, Lieutenant,} ordered the captain. *{Cass, warn the 76th they're about to have company.}*

Micah was already in motion, having anticipated the order for electronic countermeasures. His right hand pushed outward, his left simultaneously curving inward, even as Rafe spoke.

The movements weren't physical actions; as deeply enmeshed as Micah was with the ship's SyntheticVision system, they were more of a visual manifestation of his thoughts. They also resulted in immediate motion within the swarm of drones under his command.

{ECM away.}

The drones he recalled with his left hand docked silently with the ship, while the ones released by his right were flushed from several ports along *Scimitar*'s flank. Clad in the same stealth coating that enveloped the Helios, the drones were nearly impossible to detect.

Micah separated them into two swarms. One went speeding back toward the ship that was skimming across the platform's surface in its hunt for *Scimitar*. The other inserted itself between the cutter and the enemy vessel.

{Dazzlers en route, Banshees on hold,} announced Micah.

{Good. Coordinate with the coastie defense grid to avoid crossfire,} Rafe instructed.

The Dazzlers Micah had unleashed were tiny yet powerful tools in the ship's arsenal. When activated, they emitted strong electronic jamming that would deny targeting information to the enemy. The drones also blocked communication, making it impossible to coordinate an attack—and, in this case, to contact anyone who might be on the platform.

While the Dazzlers were defensive, the drones Micah held in reserve were not. Where the Dazzlers' purpose was to confuse and confound, the Banshees were built to pack a powerful punch. Their payload of missiles varied by class, and all of them mounted five-centimeter lasers that could deliver pulsed bursts of weapons fire on Micah's mental command.

{Any guesses as to who our friends out there might be?} the mental voice of *Scimitar*'s gunner tickled Micah's ear as he watched her target the tangos. The twin large-bore, RAU-19 railguns under Dana's control tracked the vessels the ship's IFF had identified as 'Foe'.

{My credit's on pirates,} Cass volunteered. *{It's no secret this platform's being decommissioned. Makes a perfect hideout—or a place to offload goods.}*

Dana scoffed. *{Well, we know one thing for sure. Whoever they are, they don't have the brains God gave a gnat. Who'd be dumb enough to go up against a Shadow Recon ship?}*

{Let's find out.} At Rafe's words, a highlight appeared on Micah's overlay. In the next instant, Rafe enlarged the image until the 'SS' icon emblazoned on the ship's ventral fin could be clearly seen.

Micah unleashed a few choice words. *{Aw, that's just great. Don't waste your time trying to persuade them to surrender. Those secessionists would rather die than give in.}*

Rafe grunted his agreement. *{Better warn the team.}*

A beat later, his voice came over the combat net. *{Noble, this is

Spartan. Tangos are SS. I say again, tangos are SS. Assume you have company, over.}

{Copy, Spartan.} Thad's voice sounded gruff, as if he were already in the thick of battle. His next words confirmed Micah's suspicions. *{Engaging.}*

The SS in the logo stood for 'Secede Sirius'. They were a separatist group that had been trying unsuccessfully for more than a century to persuade the citizens of the Sirius binary system to secede from the Geminate Alliance.

Highly nationalistic, the group's chief complaint was the imbalance of power between the two star systems of Procyon and Sirius. Their platform promised to rectify that.

The organization regularly attempted to place themselves on ballots. Sometimes it worked; most times, it didn't. They'd been around so long, few took them seriously.

That had recently changed. The SS, as they now called themselves, was under new management—one willing to use violence to make its point.

Rafe sent the Helios breaking north of the stellar plane, giving them a clear shot as the ship entered weapons range.

{Free to engage,} he said, *{but try for disabling shots if you can.}*

Micah heard Dana's reply as if from a distance. The merge he shared with the ship rendered the cockpit invisible, transmuting his perception into a different reality altogether. It was as if he floated freely in the black, his view unimpeded by something as mundane as bulkhead and hull.

Over comms, he heard Cass coordinating with the coastie defense grid, updating them in real-time of *Scimitar*'s intentions.

Scimitar surged forward. The next few minutes passed by in a blur, yet held that quality of time slowing that so often happened when senses were acute.

Although *Scimitar* was invisible to EM scans, Dana's railgun fire easily marked the Helios' location. The SS vessel returned fire, and Rafe slewed to port, tracer rounds from the enemy ship flashing by.

Micah swiveled his head to follow the other spacecraft as it began evasive maneuvers, the reticle of his Banshee's targeting app locking onto the enemy ship with smooth precision. With a thought, the drone under his command spat out a series of two-second bursts, pulsed light from its five-centimeter laser hitting the seam where the fusion drive met its powerplant.

The Banshee's initial assault weakened the area just enough that the follow-up missile Micah unleashed punched through the outer hull, severing its drive train. The other craft disintegrated instantly.

Even as the debris field expanded, Rafe was already banking *Scimitar* into a tight curve.

*{What part of **disabling** shots did you not understand, Lieutenant?}*

{That ship shouldn't have blown like it did.} Micah spared a swift glance at the man seated to his right. *{It's almost as if they had some sort of dead-man's switch wired in to ensure no prisoners were taken.}*

{Survivors?} Rafe barked the question at Cass as the ship carved an arc that took them below the plane of the system, neatly avoiding the debris field.

Out of the corner of his eye, Micah saw the crew chief shake her head. *{It must have been remotely piloted, I'm not reading any biological material in the field at all.}*

{Huh. Anyone else think this was a bit too easy?} Dana spoke into the silence.

A quick blip caught Micah's eye. At the same time, Cass let out a string of curses. *{Dana, next time, keep your damn mouth shut.}*

Three more ships swept out from behind a well-positioned asteroid whose metal content had effectively blocked their ship's scan from reading them.

{Brace for maneuvers!}

THREE

CMS GOBLIN
COBALT MINING SECTOR TWELVE

IT DIDN'T SURPRISE Katie when the ship that had nearly sideswiped *Goblin* turned its nose toward Sierra Twelve. There really wasn't anywhere else for it to go.

Space was vast, far more so than most planet-bound people realized. For another ship to have come this close to the tug was either a deliberate move by its pilot, or it was a one-in-a-million fluke. Katie was hoping it was the latter; she didn't care to think that someone wished her dead.

What really surprised her, though, was that the ship was flying dark. All vessels were required by interstellar law to have an X-Nav transponder, which used Interstellar Navigation System coordinates, to broadcast its location. INS allowed the space traffic control system and other ships in the area to know a vessel's precise location.

The near-miss that just occurred should have been impossible. And yet it had happened.

That captured Katie's curiosity.

Ordinarily, the long trek back to the platform was boring, often spent buried in homework for one of the university classes Doc had suggested she take. Not today.

After recovering the load of ore she'd ejected, she spent the transit time studying the track the ship had been on when it left the tug's sensor range, and monitoring the platform's STC channel, waiting for Sierra Twelve's sensors to grab onto the rogue ship. She entertained herself by imagining all the choice words Jeremy would have for its pilot once it neared the platform.

The real interaction came right in the middle of a song by a band called Charles or Daniels something… Katie forgot which. The music cut out precipitously, Jeremy's irate voice sounding over the feed. As she'd predicted, he immediately began to tear the pilot of the mystery spacecraft a new one.

{Ship entering Cobalt Sierra Twelve space, turn on your X-Nav!} he snapped, his tone just shy of a shout.

There was no verbal response. Thirty seconds later, Jeremy followed up with another angry spate of words.

{Unknown vessel, you are in violation of STC regs. In case you forgot,} his voice dripped sarcasm, *{that means you need to **request permission** before entering a no-wake-zone. Exit the area, check ATIS, and advise on initial contact.}*

Everyone knew to check with the Automated Traffic Information SI before entering a platform's nearspace. To do otherwise wasn't just bad manners; it was plain stupid.

When there was still no answer, Jeremy came back onto the channel, his voice sharp enough to cut glass.

*{Unmarked ship, you are in violation of STC regs. Shut down your fusion drive and exit nearspace—**now!**}*

Katie sucked in a breath at 'fusion drive'. *Goblin* was too far away for her to see anything firsthand with the tug's sensors, but she knew what Jeremy's words meant: the ship was doing the unthinkable— braking hard through Sierra Twelve's no-wake zone, in utter disregard for the safety of any other spacecraft or workers who might be in the area.

Civilian spaceships used two main forms of propulsion to move around: thrusters and fusion drives. While a thruster's compressed gases were an effective way to maneuver a ship, they did a poor job of imparting any speed. Fusion engines did the heavy lifting.

The brute force of a tokamak fusion drive could propel a ship from rest to cruising speed in very little time; it was also the fastest way to bring a ship to a stop.

The problem with that method was the fusion plant's plasma plume. The ionizing radiation it put out was lethal; that was the reason for no-wake zones. Ships coming and going from any populated region were restricted to thrusters-only, until they reached a certain distance.

From what she could hear, it sounded like this ship was placing everyone near the platform's docks in grave peril. Such a maneuver was only done under the direst of circumstances—or as an act of war.

Katie's hand rested lightly on Fred's head as she thought it through. Her fingers dug into the fur behind his right ear, absently scratching as she studied the feed on her forward display.

"*Goblin*, get me a reciprocal on the ship that nearly hit us. What was its most likely origin?"

The answer was immediate.

{The vessel appears to have originated from Cobalt Mining Platform Thirty-Seven.}

Katie frowned, her hands dancing across the console as she studied the readout the ship's SI had pushed to the main holo. "But wasn't that platform decommissioned six months ago?"

{Affirmative.}

She lapsed into silence, listening to Jeremy's increasingly irate calls, and the announcement that a pair of tugs had been scrambled to intercept the ship.

Several minutes passed, and then the channel erupted with the voices of ships' pilots raised in anger, fear, and confusion. Katie leaned forward, as if the action would help her to better discern the tangle of words. Eventually, it became clear that the strange ship had fired upon the tugs, disabling them both.

She could hear the tension in Jeremy's voice now, his words becoming ever more frantic as he ordered the ship away from Sierra Twelve.

And then, the channel fell silent.

FOUR

Abandoned Mining Platform
0.9 AU from Sierra Twelve

THAD IGNORED THE deadly battle raging in nearspace around the decommissioned platform as he prowled its empty hallways. His movements were as silent as a Ceriban hunting cat hungry for its next meal.

The prey he sought might be human by strict definition, but to the Marine's mind, anyone associated with the SS was little better than vermin, and worthy of about the same regard. His recon drones had placed them approximately a klick ahead, and moving upspin fast.

This wasn't the first decommissioned station the Unit had used for its war games, so the sight that greeted Thad when he stepped onto the platform's main concourse didn't surprise him.

Signs of hasty departure were everywhere. Conduit hung loose from dropped ceilings, where tiles had been removed for easy access. Abandoned boxes were strewn haphazardly, those who had opened them more interested in efficiency than tidiness.

He released a cloud of audio chaff to muffle the sound of his own footsteps, knowing that the platform's sound-deadening nanoacoustics had long since been stripped away. The stillness of the concourse would magnify his presence—and that of his opponent, as he closed on them.

His drakeskin suit bent the light around him, disguising his electromagnetic signature both in the visible and infrared spectrums. But a smart opponent would look for displacement in air currents, as well. He couldn't do much about that, though, so he hugged the walls, crossing from cover to cover as he progressed.

Thad had shot one of the intruders with the specially formulated paintball gun Jack had cobbled together. The impact had startled the man, and at first, he'd thought he'd been shot—only to be disabused of that notion when his partners began laughing at him.

"Is that all they have?" the man who'd been shot scoffed. "What're we waiting for, then? Let's take him down."

He'd started forward, but the man to his right grabbed his arm, pulling him to a stop. "Oh no you don't. That guy moves like real military, not like the coast guard group we took out earlier. Let's not be stupid about this, okay?"

The man shook off his restraining hand. "Then I'll be sure to let him know the favor we did for his team—right before I put a bullet between his eyes."

"Idiot," said the man on his left. "Duane's right. That prick's not moving like the coasties were. Didn't you hear what they were saying before we took 'em down? Those are Marines out there, asshole. You do *not* want to fuck with them. Now come on. Let's get back to the ship."

The man Thad had tagged wiped at his suit, casting a glare back down the corridor, to where he hid. "Easy for you to say. You're not the one with the messed-up camo."

"Shoulda zigged instead of zagged." Duane cuffed him on the back of the head.

The three moved out, and Thad let them pull further away, the microdrone he'd launched the moment the paintball hit its target floating three meters behind them, just out of earshot.

Over his suit's systems, Thad clearly heard the conversation continue as the drone transmitted the audio that the nanomaterial buried in the paintball bounced up to it. On his HUD, the spike tracker also embedded in the paint flashed a strong signal, telling him exactly where the trio was headed.

"Now, we hunt," Thad said under his breath as he superimposed the tracking ID on top of the map of the derelict platform.

He saw them turn down a stub corridor up ahead. Flattening himself against the wall, he crept toward the intersection, and nudged his drone forward as he assessed the situation.

A kiosk, its faded sign advertising 'PX Snack Bites' dangling from one corner, sat between him and his targets. It wouldn't provide much in the way of cover if the men he tracked had projectile weapons, but it would have to do.

He briefly entertained the thought of sending a drone ahead to draw their attention away from him, but discarded it almost immediately. The stub was a dead-end, and though platforms like this were notorious for the vermin they attracted, until this exercise had been scheduled, the station had been out of use for nearly six months, its atmosphere evacuated. That effectively eradicated any potential noise-makers.

Thad was willing to bet the invaders knew this, too.

He released the flap that secured his flash-bang grenades and eased his way into the corridor, his CUSP pistol sighting on the nearest IR signature. A few seconds later, he'd made it to the kiosk, and he crouched behind it.

The figures he watched were clad in an outdated form of stealth covering that his HUD's predictive systems easily identified, though he wondered how the SS had gotten their hands on military-grade equipment. More importantly, if they had the suits, what would their weapons load look like?

That decided his course of action. These *couyon* had a lot to answer for, but he'd be damned if he'd let them take pot shots at him while he questioned them.

He reached for the flash-bang, arming it with a two-second delay. Glancing down the corridor, he identified his objective: a column that protruded half a meter from the wall.

As he began his sprint, he simultaneously lobbed the grenade while triggering his drakeskin's defensive screens. Closing his eyes and opening his mouth to ward against the concussive blast, he launched himself into a low dive, rolling up against the pillar at the same instant the grenade went off.

Even through his closed eyelids and the protection his suit offered, the light was still blindingly bright. He wasted no time as it faded, knowing the disorientation brought on by the flash-bang had a finite limit.

Thad's CUSP was already up and aimed in the direction of the nearest figure. He fired, his military-grade wire implant automatically adjusting the beam's width to account for the close-in targeting solution.

He pivoted, arm extended, as he centered the weapon's reticle on the second figure, and then the third. The CUSP's beam narrowed to accommodate the more distant targets, and he fired twice more in quick succession.

All three dropped to the floor, but Thad wasn't taking any chances. He holstered the pistol and brought his rifle up from where it hung around his neck in a single-point sling. Raising the rifle's barrel to a sign hanging precariously above the two he'd just taken out, he fired several shots at the single hinge holding it in place. It landed with a crash on top of them.

Slinging the rifle back over his shoulder, he reacquired the CUSP as he advanced toward the first fallen man. He nudged the still form with his foot, and then fired one more disabling shot, center mass, to ensure the man stayed put.

Satisfied he wouldn't have to worry about his six, he closed the distance between himself and the other two, his weapon trained on the downed men.

One of them appeared to be knocked out; the other groaned and rolled to his side, attempting to shake off the effects of the CUSP. The man had to be in serious pain from the EM pulse, his nerve cells on fire. Though the setting Thad had dialed into the weapon was non-lethal, he knew from personal experience that it still hurt like a sonofabitch.

Before the man had a chance to recover, Thad took a knee beside him, pulled his hood back, and slapped a ziptie behind his left ear. Turning, he applied another to the guy's partner, and then backtracked to the first body and did the same. Now, none of the three would be able to call for help, nor move under their own volition.

The ziptie was an invasive app, one that only the military and law enforcement were legally allowed to use. It tied directly into a person's wire implant, and put the prisoner under their captor's complete control.

Thad rose, risking a brief comm burst over the combat net as he retraced his steps to the concourse. *{Three captives. Heading for extraction point.}*

Other than a two-click of acknowledgment, no reply came. That didn't worry him. The message had been received, and the team would respond in kind when they could.

Once he hit the main hall, he jogged toward a maglev cart he'd seen docked in its charging stand in an alcove set aside for such devices. As he approached, he could see that the unit wasn't fully charged.

However, its surface was coated in a TENG-PENG. The thin layer of nanogenerator batteries worked to power-harvest both the ambient sound in the atmosphere and the movement of the cart itself, converting both to stored energy.

If the platform had been operational, the cart would have been at full capacity. As it stood, with the station having been unoccupied prior to the arrival of Team Five and the coasties, the device's battery reserve had bled dry.

Thad crouched beside the unit, his right hand unsheathing the knife he kept strapped to the underside of his left wrist. Inserting the flat end of the blade against the generator that powered the maglev's coils, he pried its lid loose.

He held it open with one hand while, with the other, he opened a vest pocket and grabbed one of his CUSP's spare batteries. Peeling back the casing to expose the terminals, he tied the battery into the circuit, effectively hot-wiring it.

It hummed, the controls flickering to life. A moment later, Thad was rewarded for his efforts when the cart rose, hovering a scant centimeter above the concourse floor. Pulling it out of its charging dock, he nudged it back toward his three immobilized prisoners.

He let out a silent, relieved breath when he found them as he'd left them. He'd been careful to scan for additional SS personnel along the way, yet it always paid to be cautious.

Special forces lived by the motto, '*See one, think two.*'

While he piled the two unconscious men onto the cart, he used his wire implant to access the ziptie that held the third man immobile, altering its parameters to allow limited movement.

Stepping back, he motioned to him. "Get up."

The man glared at Thad, refusing to move.

Thad shrugged. He didn't much care whether the *couyon* walked or rode atop the pile, though he'd prefer to have the insurgent's hands occupied pushing the cart, leaving his own free to respond to any threats.

He aimed the pistol, his finger moving toward the trigger. The man rose to his feet, remembered pain causing him to respond with alacrity.

Thad motioned him over to the cart. "Push."

He followed behind as his captive pushed the maglev through the concourse. Halfway to the hatch where the team had inserted, Lane's voice sounded in his head.

{Noble Two. Noble Three and Five are en route and will rendezvous with you.}

He sent her a quick two-click to acknowledge.

{Noble Four and Six, head to alternate LZ. Our hosts will guide you in.}

A flurry of two-clicks followed from each of the other team members.

Unit protocol dictated such brevity as a way to keep the enemy from triangulating a location through comm transmissions. The likelihood of the SS being able to track them was nonexistent; still, SOP was followed.

Thad's eyes strayed to the slumped forms on the maglev cart, clad in decades-old Navy stealth suits. Someone out there was supplying these *fils-putain* with military-grade equipment, despite its age.

Maybe it's best not to underestimate these people.

As he drew near the airlock leading to the maintenance hatch, he caught sight of Jack and Asha, code-named Noble Three and Noble Five.

"LT," the Marine intelligence officer greeted, and Thad lifted his chin in response. Asha gave Thad a silent nod, her eyes watchful as she kept her weapon trained down the corridor.

The curious light in Jack's eyes told Thad the intelligence officer wanted to ask about the pile of bodies piled atop the maglev cart, once they were back aboard *Scimitar*.

"Later," he warned, and Jack nodded.

Asha slung her rifle over her shoulder, unclipping the scanner at her waist as she approached the cart.

"Those two will be coming out from under a CUSP soon," Thad informed her as she reached for the first man. "They're also ziptied." He touched her wrist lightly with one hand, initiating a peer-to-peer connection between their wires, allowing him to transfer the two zipties to her control.

She acknowledged the handover even as her eyes remained fixed on her patients.

"Wonder where they got these," Jack murmured, fingering the cloth of one of the stealth suits the men wore.

Though it was several generations old, it was still far superior to anything on the civilian market. If this platform had been occupied by Cobalt employees, they would have had no way to detect the infiltration, and no warning before a surprise attack.

"That's one of the things we need to find out," replied Thad, pinning Jack with a wordless look.

Jack's lips tightened in response to the unspoken order as Thad held up a palm. Jack clasped it in an upright grip, and Thad used the contact to hand over control of the third man.

The slow smile that creased Jack's face as he turned to face the insurgent was the stuff of nightmares.

He advanced, one hand releasing the holster that secured his flechette, while the other beckoned the man forward. "You. Come with me." Jack's eyes had gone dead, his voice held the whisper of death. He looked like he'd just as soon shoot the guy as interrogate him.

The SS separatist fought the Ziptie with all his might, but to no avail. He swallowed convulsively when Jack snapped his fingers, his body lurching forward under the app's compulsion.

"Inside," Jack ordered, pointing to the airlock.

Thad suspected the man thought he was about to be spaced.

Jack dipped his head to Thad, and the lieutenant caught a twinkle of amusement in the other Marine's eyes before he turned and followed his prisoner inside, the hatch cycling shut behind him.

Asha blew out a breath. "He can be scary as hell when he does that, you know?"

A deep chuckle shook Thad's frame. "All part of the routine. He gets into their heads and fucks with them. If it helps save lives, I'm all for it, *cher.*"

Fifteen minutes later, Jack emerged, all traces of humor gone.

"We need to round up the rest of the team and get the hell off this platform."

Asha's head jerked up. "Is the team in danger?"

Jack shook his head. "Not them, no. Ironically enough, these jokers were here for much the same reason we were… except their war games were a rehearsal for a very real hostage situation going down on a nearby platform—and it's already underway."

* * *

The ships that emerged from behind the asteroid had a clear agenda. Micah had to admit it would have been an effective strategy, if they hadn't been up against a Shadow Recon ship and its crew.

While two of the ships harried *Scimitar,* the third bolted for the black.

{Spike him!} Rafe's order slashed through Micah's head even as he spun out three Griffins and sent them arrowing at the fleeing vessel.

{On it.}

The stealth drones that sped after the escaping craft were all sleek speed, rolled up into an impressively covert package. Their small but mighty fusion reactors were hidden behind layers of high-performance electromagnetic shielding. Their cross-sectional return was so small, even standard Navy ships' SIs would dismiss them as a blip from a system's heliospheric current sheet.

Buried amidst its twisted graphene-and-foam substrates, each drone carried one very powerful tool: a program that would 'spike' its objective with a shower of nanoscopic tags. Identical to the spike Jack had integrated into the paintball pellets, each tag held a unique geometric signature, registered in a secured special operations database.

An app aboard each drone would register the negative space created by each spike on the surface it tagged, and track the void, pinpointing its location.

The ship the Griffins were pursuing was boosting hard, and Micah had to accelerate the drones to fifty *g*s before they reached an overfly velocity. By the time they neared their objective, the drones were already far enough out to account for several seconds of light lag, so Micah handed control over to each drone's SI.

He kept one eye on the feed while he returned his attention to the two ships *Scimitar* was engaging. Rafe flipped the ship, giving Dana an oblique shot at one of the vessels' more vulnerable forward thruster ports. She obligingly strafed the craft with railgun fire as

Scimitar shot past, the engagement over almost before it had begun.

Rafe flipped once again, braking hard to counteract momentum, as Micah's attention locked onto the second ship. It was doing its best to keep its port side toward *Scimitar*, which suggested damage somewhere along its starboard sidewalls.

Micah snuck a pair of Banshees above the vessel while Dana distracted it with a broadside. His lips curved into a predatory smile as he saw he'd guessed correctly.

He unleashed the drones' five-centimeter lasers in short, deadly pulses at the damaged section, and then stopped abruptly as the ship veered sharply away, heavily venting atmosphere.

{Open comm,} Rafe ordered.

A beat later, Micah heard Cass's voice.

{Comm open, sir.}

Rafe ordered the ship to heave to, and when it looked like the ship would comply, Micah returned his focus to the spiked ship.

{SS vessels, prepare to be boarded}, he heard Rafe say as a pair of Novastrike attack crafts launched from the coast guard cutter and began to close on the two disabled enemy ships.

{I've got a solid lock on the third ship,} Micah announced, flipping the data up onto the ship's net.

{Good. Let's leave cleanup to the cutter. Ping the team and tell them we're hunting down that third—}

Cass cut Rafe off. *{Sir, you need to hear this.}*

Lane broke through, her voice terse. *{Request pickup ASAP. Intel suggests SS is engaging a nearby platform.}*

{Shit. You mean they're that organized, and Navy Intelligence hasn't caught onto it yet?}

{Would appear so, yes.}

{On our way,} Rafe told Lane as he maneuvered *Scimitar* back toward the platform.

{Good copy, Scimitar. Coasties'll handle things here so we can move on to the next objective.}

Micah's ears pricked up at that. *{You have a bead on their planned hit?}* he interjected.

{Yes.} Thad's voice picked up where Lane left off. *{Scimitar and Team Five are the nearest responders, so we're up. We'll need to proceed with caution… sounds like it's a hostage situation.}*

FIVE

CMS *GOBLIN*
COBALT MINING SECTOR TWELVE

KATIE SPENT A tense few hours waiting to hear from Jeremy… or anyone from Sierra Twelve, for that matter. Once STC fell silent, she brought up the channel that the pilots used to converse between ships. There was a lot of chatter and speculation on what was going on—more activity than she'd ever heard, in fact—but no real news.

Pilots nearest to the platform were recounting what they'd seen in a play-by-play manner, while the ships farthest away plied them with questions. Theories were bandied back and forth, everything from pirates to a top-secret government operation, although the guy who'd suggested that last had been ribbed pretty hard for it.

When the STC channel came to life once more, it wasn't Jeremy's voice she heard.

{All ships are to return to Sierra Twelve. Repeat, all ships, return to Sierra Twelve.}

The single order was transmitted, repeated once, and then the channel went dark. The unfamiliar voice would not reply to any of the pilots' queries.

The platform had just entered the envelope, the extreme reach of *Goblin*'s sensor range. It looked different somehow, and Katie studied it, wondering what it was that seemed out of place. Abruptly, she realized the difference was that there were more ships docked at the platform than she was used to seeing in one place.

For some reason, the ships that had been scheduled to depart were being held back. She'd be crossing over into Sierra Twelve's nearspace soon, and officially under its area of influence.

If the platform was in trouble, and she could do something to help, she would have to make her move very soon. Yet, she didn't want to make a hasty decision she ended up regretting. Before taking any action, she decided to reach out to a nearby platform to see if she could learn anything about the mysterious ship.

"*Goblin*, connect to Sierra Twelve's Starshot buoy, and get me Platform Twenty-Nine's STC Center."

There was a pause, and then the ship responded. *{Unable to comply. Ford-Svaiter node unavailable.}*

Katie sat up in alarm. In all her eighteen years, she'd never once heard of a Ford-Svaiter node going down.

"*Goblin*, try again."

The response was the same.

Eyes narrowing in thought, she ordered the ship to connect to a more distant Starshot buoy, located an AU beyond Sierra Twelve, on the rimward side.

Goblin's response was the same.

She frowned. "Well, that makes about as much sense as a trap door in a tokamak."

The odds of one node being down were very low. The odds of two nodes being down bordered on the incomprehensible.

"*Goblin*, try the Starshot buoy toward Heliodor."

{Negative reception. Ford-Svaiter node unavailable.}

If three nodes were down, then whoever had arrived on Sierra Twelve must actively be jamming the frequencies. The newcomers were hostile.

Now she needed to figure out what she was going to do about it.

SIX

GNS *SCIMITAR*

EN ROUTE

COBALT PLATFORM SIERRA TWELVE

Several hours earlier....

THOSE ABOARD *SCIMITAR* endured a hard, fifty-*g* accel for the first two hours of flight time. This allowed the Helios to catch up with the spiked vessel, Rafe maneuvering them into the optimal position to follow without being spotted. Once they'd reached that point, they eased off, matching the other ship's two-*g* burn as they followed silently at a distance.

Micah wasn't sure he agreed with the instructions Lane had received from Colonel Valenti, back at SRU headquarters in Procyon. The colonel had ordered them to follow but not engage until there was clear evidence that the SS had taken the platform and was holding its employees hostage.

{Technically, we're not supposed to be operating within our own borders at all,} Jack reminded them when Dana voiced what they'd

all been thinking. *{We're the Alliance's military force, remember? Not its peacekeeping one.}*

{Tell that to anyone who gets shot and killed while we sit on our asses and watch,} grumbled Cass.

{Not disagreeing with you, there, cher,} Thad supplied, *{but for some reason, HQ keeps forgetting to ask my opinion about the orders they give.}*

That got a snort out of Cass. *{Point,}* she admitted. *{But that doesn't mean we have to like it, all the same.}*

{Ooh-rah,} Mike muttered from where he sat reclined in one of the cabin seats, his cap pulled low over his brow. *{Wake me when there are SS assholes to blow up.}*

From there, it was a long, tedious journey, *Scimitar* lagging far enough behind not to be picked up on the ship's sensors. When it became clear the ship was headed to Sierra Twelve, Lane had them diverge from the flight path for a close pass by the sector's Starshot buoy, just long enough for Cass to download recordings of the area from the past few days. The data would allow the team to get the lay of the land before they approached.

The SRU team huddled around a portable console, poring over the logs for the next hour. Micah deployed a small swarm of drones while *Scimitar* floated in space beside the buoy, awaiting her passengers' instructions. He also kept a surface connection with the drones following the SS ship.

He pulled out of the connection long enough to focus his attention fully on Lane when the SRU team captain swiveled her chair around to face the cockpit.

An icon began to flash in the lower corner of the forward screens, indicating a file was being pushed to it. Rafe reached for it, and the icon expanded into a map of the nearby asteroid wall that formed the edge of the Cobalt Outback.

"Their destination," Lane told them with a head-tilt indicating the flashing pin she'd dropped on a nearby mining platform. "Sierra Twelve has six thousand residents, give or take, servicing three main rigs buried deep within the wall. They—"

A proximity warning began to sound from the Griffin drones following the SS ship, cutting her off mid-sentence.

Micah jerked his head around at the sound, his senses plunging deep into the interface. He wasn't with the ship any longer; he was one hundred thousand kilometers away, shadowing a ship running dark, and barreling toward an unsuspecting Cobalt Mining tug.

"Report, Lieutenant," Rafe's voice sounded as if from a great distance.

{Turn, you fool,} Micah's mental voice went out over the shipnet. *{Turn!}*

{Lieutenant Case!}

Micah flipped the feed onto *Scimitar*'s main screens, his entire focus on the two converging ships. He let out a gust of air when the tug released its load and bolted stellar south, the ship's overpowered drives giving it an enormous boost. Still, it was barely enough.

The other ship executed a hard turn, momentum carrying it dangerously close to the netted sphere of rocks. Somehow, it managed to evade, though Micah had to wonder about the condition of its paint job afterward.

His mind registered exclamations from the crew with some detachment, their reactions as they watched the near-miss play out, but his focus was pinned to the two ships. When he was convinced neither had come to harm, he pulled out of the SyntheticVision merge.

Mike's was the first voice he heard clearly. "Think I might need to go change my shorts, after that."

Rafe shook his head, voice tinged with disgust. "With the SS ship flying dark, that tug had virtually no warning until they were almost on top of it. That was some quick thinking by the pilot."

Micah nodded. "Agreed."

They resumed their watchful waiting, the hours ticking down until the ship would arrive in Sierra Twelve's nearspace.

Fifteen hours and counting.

SEVEN

CMS *GOBLIN*

COBALT MINING SECTOR TWELVE

KATIE STARED OUT the tug's airlock window, at the platform floating several hundred kilometers in the distance. The station seemed so very far away. It wouldn't be her first non-tethered EVA, but it would certainly be the first time she'd ever purposely turned off her suit's locator beacon.

It had become painfully clear over the past several hours that something was seriously wrong with Sierra Twelve. The unfamiliar voice that had come over the STC channel and demanded all Cobalt ships to return to the platform had fallen silent.

To say this was highly irregular was an understatement. First, Cobalt Mining didn't shut down for anything short of a massive solar event from Big Blue, which meant its STC was always talking to one ship or another.

Second, the mandate was impossible to follow. Many of the ships were on weeks-long deployments, the kind her father used to fly. There was no conceivable way they could comply.

She'd initially ignored the order herself, but had been called harshly to task when she'd failed to change her heading. Knowing a gut reaction wasn't the most reliable navaid, she'd reluctantly turned her nose back toward Sierra Twelve.

Besides, it wasn't like she had anywhere else she could go; *Goblin* wasn't equipped for long-haul trips. Although enviro could handle it, there certainly wasn't enough food to sustain both her and Fred for the three-plus days it would take her to get to the next platform.

If there was something going on, she'd need to gather evidence before she made her escape.

Katie had tried raising Doc to see if he knew anything about what was going on, but he hadn't answered. This wasn't unusual, though; he often put his wire on Do Not Disturb while seeing patients.

Jeremy hadn't answered either, when she'd first tried to contact him on a private channel. She tried again an hour later, and then again an hour after that. The third time, she finally got through, but his voice sounded strained and awkward, and it set her spidey senses tingling.

When he'd asked how her *cat* was doing, she'd known for sure something was wrong. Jeremy knew all about Fred; he'd been known to slip the pup a rawhide bone from time to time.

So now here she stood, at *Goblin*'s aft airlock, suited up for an EVA that broke all the rules. She'd forced herself to think through all the options, and this one, while risky, provided her with the best chance for successfully sneaking onto Sierra Twelve without anyone the wiser.

And maybe, just maybe, she'd be able to send out a call for help in the process.

Katie's ID was currently listed with Sierra Twelve's SI as being aboard *Goblin*. If her ruse was going to work, they needed to continue to think she was aboard the tug—certainly not arrowing her way through the black toward a little-used maintenance hatch.

She also knew that if she allowed the platform to register her presence, the control center would be notified immediately. So she'd disabled her wire's auto-connect feature, as well.

Two super dumb things a pilot was taught never, ever to do. Yeah, she was breaking *all* the rules.

She looked down at the rounded bump protruding from her EVA suit, where Fred lay tucked against her belly. The pup wriggled and whined, unhappy with his confinement.

"Just a little while longer," she told him as she retested the integrity of her suit's seal one last time.

Everything read green.

She'd checked the radiation sensors mounted on *Goblin*'s hull, and read the latest space weather report just before suiting up. Today's measurements were well within the safe range for the amount of time she'd be outside the ship—for a human.

The risks to Fred were greater, she knew. He was a puppy and still developing. Unfortunately, she didn't know how great a risk, so getting Fred to medical so Doc Slater could check him out would be her top priority once she made it to the platform.

She palmed the hatch open and felt a brief gust of wind as the tiny airlock's atmosphere evacuated. Fred squirmed as her suit compensated for the vacuum. Checking that her bag of supplies was secured to its tether, she planted her boots against the edge of the hatch and pushed off.

As the tug fell away behind her, Katie brought up a visual approach indicator that showed both heading and distance to destination on her overlay. The numbers spiraled down the closer she got to the access hatch. After several seconds of monitoring her heading, Katie switched her attention to the tug.

Rotating her body to keep *Goblin* in her line of sight, she tested the whiskerbeam she'd set up prior to departure. The untraceable tightbeam connection would allow her to continue the pretense that she was still aboard the tug. It also allowed her to send *Goblin*'s SI instructions remotely.

Katie waited until her readout showed she was safely out of range. Once assured she wouldn't be caught in the tug's plasma wash, she initiated a starboard thruster burn, turning the ship's nose away from the platform.

As expected, the change in heading elicited a sharp response from the person who had taken over STC.

{Cobalt tug Goblin, *correct your heading,}* the voice instructed.

{Sorry about that, Sierra Twelve. I've developed a bit of a hitch in my git-along. Hang on, trying to stabilize.}

She reckoned the more confusion she could toss into the mix, the better, so she leavened her speech with a heavy dose of platform slang. She doubted whoever was on the other end was too familiar with the patois.

She also figured they'd lose patience with the tug, and order it to turn back soon. While she waited, she split her attention between the ship and her destination, watching the spar grow larger as she neared it.

The silence lasted all of thirty seconds.

{Goblin, correct your course now!}

Katie keyed the comms and let out a long, audible sigh. *{Sorry 'bout that, Sierra Twelve. You know these things turn about as fast as a herd o' turtles. You don't want me to lose this net full of stones, now, do ya? You know the quartermaster; he's as tight as a bull's ass at fly time.}*

Her offer to ditch what was arguably a high-value load of metals should have resulted in a quick refusal, but it didn't. That was telling.

She only had to stretch this drama out another five minutes. At that point, she could trigger the distraction that would cover her suit's braking burn so she didn't end up splattered against the platform's hull.

She altered *Goblin*'s course this way and that as she continued the charade with STC. As the clock hit the five-minute mark, she pulled up a stack of preset instructions she'd programmed to execute on her command, swiftly scanning through them one last time.

It's now or never.

{Goblin, execute operation Asshat One.}

{Compliance,} came the voice of the ship's SI.

Instantly, the grapples securing *Goblin*'s cargo released. As the netted asteroid chunks floated free, the now-unfettered tug nosed down below the plane, braking hard.

The maneuver dropped the ship neatly behind the material it had so recently been hauling. With a wall of rock now between it and the platform, *Goblin*'s fusion drives went to maximum thrust.

Katie imagined she could hear the drives screaming as the tug tried to claw its way back along the reciprocal of its course, its velocity slowly increasing as it overcame its previous momentum. She sent the stolid little tug a mental apology at the abuse it was taking as she fired her own suit's thrusters, confident that whoever was in the STC was well-occupied looking the other way.

As she'd predicted, the tug's unexpected movements took the terrorists by surprise. What she hadn't anticipated was that it would also draw their fire. If she wanted to get her SOS out, Katie realized she'd better send her final command to the ship.

She fancied she saw a slight puff of air escape as a modified probe was propelled from one of the tug's starboard sensor ports. Ordinarily used for materials assays, Katie had modified this one, fitting it with a small logic cube. It held all of the information *Goblin* had gathered on the unknown ship, as well as a summary of the current situation on the mining platform.

The powerful emission from the tug's drives hid the probe's smaller EM profile, and Katie kept it on the same heading so that *Goblin* would continue to mask its presence from those who had taken over Sierra Twelve.

She'd programmed the probe to fly dark once ejected from the vessel. With its transponder off, nothing but its own engine wash could give its presence away.

It would continue to boost silently along the same path as the tug until it passed beyond Sierra Twelve's sensors and weapons range. She'd made a wild guess on the intruders' jamming equipment, and was hoping its reach wasn't much more than what the platform could achieve.

Her body remained tense while the numbers flashing in red on her overlay spun down. The minute the probe hit the safe zone and the numbers turned green, the probe's transponder came online. She let out a whoop as and it began transmitting a Mayday signal on all channels.

She smiled viciously. *That oughta jerk a knot in your tail, you egg-suckin' pieces a' owl shit.*

Her smile fell from her face moments later as a missile streaked from the platform's dock.

EIGHT

GNS *SCIMITAR*

NEARING PLATFORM SIERRA TWELVE

THE MOMENT *SCIMITAR*'S crew realized the SS vessel wasn't going to abide by the no-wake rules, they had a decision to make. Doing the same meant revealing their presence, and neither Lane nor Rafe wanted to lose the advantage of secrecy.

Aside from that was the issue of Sierra Twelve's own safety. The Secede Sirius ship's actions demonstrated a complete disregard for the lives of those on the platform. The warriors on board the Helios weren't about to add to that.

Rafe began to brake outside the no-wake-zone, allowing the SS ship to surge ahead. By the time the tug began its fateful run, *Scimitar* was too far out of range to be of any assistance to the tug's pilot, even with the Banshees Micah had already deployed into a forward array.

They'd listened in on the frequency, had all heard the exchange between the girl piloting the tug and the platform. Whoever she was, she sounded like a spirited individual—and far too young to be going head to head with the likes of the SS.

A sick feeling punched Micah in the gut when railfire from the platform's defense systems raked *Goblin*'s fuselage from tip to stern. The tug jinked erratically, but it was hopeless. Eventually, the platform's guns got in a strike, and the punctured hull vented atmosphere in one huge gout.

Micah heard someone's breath hiss out in an explosive gasp. Thad let loose a string of Cajun expletives, while inside his head, Cass's mental voice did much the same.

{Someone tell me that girl had the smarts to suit up before she began her run,} Lane said. Micah heard anger in her voice, and knew it wasn't directed at the tug, but at the heartless bastards shooting at an unarmed vessel.

*{Micah, is there **any** chance your drones can—}* Jack's words were hoarse with strain, and he cut off abruptly when he saw the slight shake of Micah's head.

{I could target the platform's railguns, but if I were to miss....} Micah didn't need to complete the thought. Everyone knew what that meant, and the risk to civilians was just too high.

{The Banshees' onboard SIs can't get targeting solutions on the railfire quickly enough to use their lasers to neutralize the projectiles,} he added. *{They'd get some, but not all.}*

Lane shook her head. *{It would also give away our presence, and we'd lose every tactical advantage we have.}*

{It's a no-win scenario.} Ell's voice intruded quietly into the conversation.

Micah agreed. *{The only good thing about this situation is I don't have to bother hiding the Banshees' emissions. Those damn fools are lighting up that little spot in the black with so much EM, there's no way those dicks can spot them.}*

A warning ping on *Scimitar*'s defensive systems sounded, the tone indicating a missile had been detected.

{What the hell?}

{Where'd that come fr—}

{Platforms aren't equipped with—}

*{Oh **shiiiiit**.}*

The cacophony of voices cut off as the tug erupted in a large cloud of fire and vaporized gases, and silence fell upon those inside *Scimitar.*

Asha's voice broke the quiet. The medic's soft declaration was layered with guilt, anger, and the sense of powerlessness they all felt.

{She was just a kid, for star's sake.}

* * *

Scimitar continued on its least-time intercept with the platform, the Unit warriors conferring in quiet, intense tones as they determined the best location to infiltrate without being seen.

Micah pulled himself out of the moody funk he'd fallen into after the destruction of the defenseless tug, when Lane straightened and pivoted toward the cockpit.

{We'll insert here.}

The Unit commander pushed an image to Rafe, who dropped it onto the forward holoscreens. A pulsing icon indicated a spot on one of the platform's spars.

Rafe enlarged the image as Lane began to lay out the plan for them.

{That access hatch is at the end of the southernmost spar. Not a whole lot down that way, mostly warehouses and a few auxiliary powerplants. It dumps directly into the maintenance tunnels. From there, we'll have our choice of any number of ingress points.}

Lane sat back and pinned an expectant look on Jack, who nodded and took up the briefing.

{It'll also give me plenty of time to infiltrate their systems. What I gleaned from your buoy download,} the intelligence officer inclined his head toward Cass, *{suggests that the platform's OS is at least two generations behind most modern Cobalt Mining rigs. Their physical infrastructure's so out of date, they're forced to run a legacy system. Should be easy to hack.}*

Rafe scraped a hand along his chin, his eyes thoughtful as they shifted between Cass and Jack. *{Cass will establish our own backdoor, as per SOP. We'll monitor you as best we can, give you backup if you need it.}*

Jack lifted a chin toward Rafe in thanks. *{You have an ETA?}*

Micah looked at the ship's telemetry; they'd entered the no-wake zone a few hours earlier.

{Another hour before we reach the spar,} Rafe told them. *{Call it…another half hour after that before we arrive at the hatch.}*

Lane nodded and turned back to the team. *{Gear check in thirty.}*

* * *

Katie's heart hurt when the tug exploded in a flash of heat, light, and expanding gases.

Sorry, Goblin. *You were a good ship….*

She shook herself, resolutely averting her eyes from the sight. She'd done all she could; now it was time to focus on her imminent arrival.

Her eyes remained fixed on the spar as the distance indicator spooled downward and her velocity continued to decrease. Her feet touched down beside the maintenance hatch with a little more force than she'd intended, but she was ready for it and immediately activated the magnetic soles in her boots.

In the next instant, Katie slammed the canister in her gloved hand onto the hatch's palmpad. The action triggered a Crowbar she'd customized and coded herself.

The code wasn't technically legal, but it was something most Cobalt miners kept on the data partition of their wire implants. Working on an older mining platform meant occasionally bumping into antiquated equipment that required a hack in order to get it up and running again. It had been a simple matter to transfer it to a small canister of nano formation material she kept in her toolkit aboard *Goblin.*

The preprogrammed hack insinuated itself into the system, overriding its security lock within seconds. Another, slightly more sophisticated program followed on its heels, bypassing the platform SI's monitoring systems. If she'd done her work correctly, the hatch would continue to register as closed, and no one would know she'd arrived.

Katie moved swiftly the moment the hatch cycled open, pulling herself inside and reeling her tethered bag in behind her. She dropped lightly onto the airlock's metal deck, relieved to once more feel the influence of artificial gravity, generated by the platform's spin. Keying the outer hatch shut behind her, she crossed to the inner hatch, footsteps ringing in the airlock's long, narrow confines.

Anyone used to the modern conveniences of a torus-shaped space station would find the configuration between the inner and outer hatches a bit unusual. The thing was oddly shaped, only three meters wide, but more than seven long.

She knew the distance she traversed was the thickness imparted by a meters-thick water bladder, inserted just beneath the platform's outer hull. It was an old-school way of providing an extra measure of protection against ionizing radiation, both from galactic solar rays and the particles flung from Sirius' main star.

Water shields fell out of use once the new, modular magnetospheres were invented. Plasma-tube-fed artificial magnetospheres were much more reliable, and designed in such a way that if one sector were to fail, the overlapping sectors on either side could easily compensate until the failed tube was repaired and brought back online.

There's a lot about Sierra Twelve that's old-school, she thought as she eyed the worn palmpad embedded in the bulkhead above the inner airlock.

She planned on taking advantage of that fact as much as she could.

Katie curled her hand protectively around Fred as the pup wriggled to be set free. He whined, a small, high-pitched noise, and she shushed him with a comforting murmur.

"Hang on, little dude. You'll be out soon."

Stripping her gloves from her hands, she danced her fingers over the palmpad, entering a hack she'd introduced into the platform's systems back when she was still a preteen.

The backdoor was something she checked periodically; old habit, not that she ever used it. She was thankful now that she'd bothered to maintain it.

Her first action was to trigger a subroutine that would tell the SIs that maintained Sierra Twelve to look the other way where the maintenance tunnels were concerned.

Nothing to see here, move along.

That done, she reached for the inner airlock, but then paused, her hand hovering over the plate. There was no real way to know if anyone was on the other side, since Cobalt hadn't deemed the tunnels important enough to monitor with sensors.

She sucked in a lungful of air, gave a small, decisive nod, and then whispered, "Here goes nothing...."

* * *

Scimitar was closing in on its target. For the past ten minutes, the team had been crowded silently around the aft airlock. Mike was the only one inside, his drakeskin suit sealed against the vacuum of space.

In one hand, the demolitions expert held a Bravo Charlie. The other was poised above the controls for the outer hatch, ready to cycle it and deploy the umbilical that would secure *Scimitar* to the platform's hull.

Micah was watching from outside, his connection to the drones giving him an up-close view of the airlock as the ship eased closer. It stopped scant centimeters from the opening. He saw the demolitions expert reach out with the breaching canister, and then freeze.

{We have a problem.}

{Sitrep,} Lane barked, and Micah could hear the Unit operator expel his breath as he pulled his hand away from the hatch.

{Someone beat us to it,} he announced. *{This hatch has been*

breached, and recently. I'm seeing evidence of a crude Crowbar, but then it's overlaid by some sort of homemade hack that I—}

{Don't touch that!} Jack shouted, and Micah heard a flurry of movement as the intelligence officer sealed his own drakeskin and joined his teammate inside the airlock.

The crew waited silently for Jack's assessment. When it came, it only added another layer of complexity to an already charged situation.

{This doesn't carry the same signature as anything the SS has used in the past,} Jack said slowly. {It's like it's been cobbled together by someone self-taught. There are parts of this that are freaking brilliant, actually, but—}

{Campbell,} Lane's voice cut in. {Will they be able to tell we're here if Mike applies the Bravo Charlie? Do we need to seek another location to breach?}

{Sorry.} The fascination in Jack's voice had muted, his tone once more crisp and professional. {No, ma'am. We should be good to enter here. But the BC isn't technically necessary. Someone's already applied a bypass to the platform's sensors.}

{Do it anyway. And I want this intruder found.}

NINE

SIERRA TWELVE
AUXILIARY ENVIRONMENTAL PLANT

THE RATTLE AND wheeze of the pipes threading through Sierra Twelve's auxiliary enviro plant was a familiar sound. Its humidity was less familiar, although it was a welcome change from the perpetual chill that permeated the unheated maintenance tunnels.

This had been Katie's hideout when she was younger. Today, it would play a strategic role as she went about planning her attack.

Her first step was to ensure that neither she nor Fred were in danger of discovery. She unsealed her suit and set Fred on his feet, securing his magnetic leash to a nearby pipe. Then she ducked out to do a quick recon of the tunnels that ran nearby.

She checked every access point that led from the tunnels into the platform's living spaces—and found nothing.

Katie allowed herself a small, satisfied grin. The invaders either didn't know about the tunnels—which was totally dumb, because maintenance tunnels were everywhere—or they didn't see them as a threat.

Their mistake.

When she returned to Fred, he acted as if she'd left him for days rather than minutes, pawing at her ecstatically and making pitiful whining noises that made her roll her eyes.

"Drama much?" she whispered, taking his little face between her hands and rubbing his ears. "Now, be good. And *stay quiet* while I check on one more thing. Then we'll go see Doc, okay?"

Fred wiggled energetically and gave another whine, recognizing the name of the platform's medical officer—someone who often slipped him treats under the table.

"Yeah, I know. Your favorite human." She booped him on the nose and set his front paws back down on the ground. "Now remember, quiet, or no visit."

She had no idea if Fred understood her or not, but the puppy obediently circled twice and then flopped to the ground with a little whuffing sound.

Satisfied he'd remain silent for at least the next few minutes, Katie moved over to a seemingly blank section of bulkhead, behind which was stashed her equipment.

As a teen, she had come across a supply of raw, unused ActiveFiber material, the kind used to line the interiors of ships and other, smaller space habitats. It had taken weeks' worth of research, of combing the public net and requesting data sheets from industrial libraries on Heliodor, before she fully grasped how versatile the material truly was.

Aside from reclaiming waste and repurposing it, ActiveFiber was capable of reshaping itself into any form a person could devise. Imagination was one thing Katie had in abundance, so she'd whiled away many hours in the privacy of her hideaway, learning how to manipulate the material. With a bit of trial and error, she concocted a skim coating, keyed to her palmprint, that she could use to mask an access panel, behind which she'd hidden her belongings.

Now, she reached out to rest her palm against the blank wall, and the material beneath it began to move. The coating retreated, thickening into a border that was the same shade of battleship gray as the bulkhead it rested upon. The access panel it revealed squeaked on its hinges as she opened it, and she made a mental note to lubricate it before she left.

The cubby inside held all the things a younger Katie had treasured: a pilfered stash of meal ration bars, a few bottles of water, and data cubes filled with her favorite shows from several years past. Blankets and cushions were tucked around her stash, the essentials for her own private home away from home.

Her most prized possession, though, was a console she'd rescued from a recycle bin and painstakingly restored. She blew a layer of dust from the tarp covering it and removed it from the cubby. Her fingers traced over its surface, the familiar shape fitting comfortably in her hands as she set it on top of a nearby crate she'd upcycled into a makeshift table.

Placing her hand on the palmpad, she smiled when the creaky old thing came to life.

The screen itself was a simple 2-D affair, an antiquated biocrystal display that dated back to the colony ships. It didn't matter; it still functioned and was perfectly capable of delivering the information she needed.

She dragged over an old chair and tried to dust off the cushion, succeeding only in smearing the dirt with her sweaty hand. With a shrug, she wiped the grime off onto her shipsuit's pantleg and took a seat in front of the unit.

Katie carefully navigated her way through the virtual keyboard projected by the console, slowly picking up speed as she refamiliarized herself with this old form of communication. She experienced a moment of regret that she'd never gotten around to installing a wireless connection to her own evanescent wire implant, but she'd lost interest in the project after her father's death.

She shoved the painful memory back where it belonged—in the past—and focused on the task before her.

One of the endeavors she was most proud of during her years of learning to understand and map the code underpinning the platform's operating system was the hack she'd managed to insinuate into the secured communications of the control room via the platform's public net. She'd perfected it when she was thirteen.

At the time, she'd been sorely tempted to tell her father about her accomplishment, knowing he'd be proud, but she had worried he'd ban her from using it.

In order for the backdoor she'd set in place to work, she'd had to find a way to disguise it, hiding it in plain sight and forcing those maintaining the network to dismiss it as an irregular system glitch that popped up from time to time—annoying, yet harmless.

The wheeze and clank of the auxiliary enviro room was what had given her the inspiration, so she'd tied it to that. Each time the unit kicked in—and Katie had mapped how often it did—her system would introduce a low-powered carrier wave masked as RF interference into the control room's comm channel.

To her surprise, it had worked beautifully. She'd been able to eavesdrop on official conversations, and never got caught. As a kid, she'd listen in for hours, especially on days when her dad was due back, hoping to hear his voice over the STC channel.

Now, the auxiliary environmental unit roared to life as she established access to her backdoor, just as it had so many times before. She wasted no time. She slipped through the network, insinuating herself into the control room.

What she saw there confirmed her worst fears. Ten men and women, heavily armed, stood watch over the platform manager and his first shift team, including Jeremy. A few of the stations were empty, though; she wondered about that.

As she watched, an alert sounded on the workstation that held the network's control interface.

One of the armed men stepped forward, gesturing threateningly at the woman who crewed that console. "What the hell is that?"

The woman moved to silence the alarm, but froze, hand extended, when the man fired his weapon. Katie heard the metallic *ting!* of the bullet that skimmed just past the woman's head, impacting a corner of the console.

"You move only when I say you can," ordered the terrorist.

"Now, tell me what that alarm signifies."

The platform's manager stepped forward cautiously, and Katie saw half a dozen rifle barrels snap up, trained on him.

He raised his hands, palms forward, in a gesture of supplication. "It's an old alert." He cleared his voice nervously. "We get an RF interference bleed every time the auxiliary and viral plant comes online. It's been this way for literally five years, and we've been unable to trace it."

Katie saw the man holding them hostage narrow his eyes suspiciously. She could practically taste the tension in the air as the manager continued.

"It's true. Headquarters said it was too expensive to replace, but we can't do without a backup, so we've just had to work around it as best we can."

The man holding the gun on the woman at the console gave her a sharp look, and she nodded timidly, confirming the manager's explanation.

"I can show you, if you wish," she offered, voice shaking.

He motioned with his weapon for her to continue, and she pointed to her display, pulling up a schematic of the platform and zeroing in on the warren of maintenance tunnels that wove throughout.

"The interference is being generated by unshielded equipment in the auxiliary enviro unit. It's located at the base of this spar, here."

The area flashed as she highlighted it.

"Indira, check it out."

One of the women holding a weapon on the manager brought her gun to its high ready position at the snapped order, then stepped toward the control room's doors.

"Hold on," one of the armed men protested. "We already have Agnew and DeVries patrolling the plant, Grayson and Smalls in lodging, and Zeff, Todds, and Moran on the dock. You really want to stretch us that thin?"

"You trying to tell me how to run this op, Gardner?"

"No, man. C'mon." He gestured around at the seated Cobalt

employees. "Isn't everyone on the platform accounted for? If they're not out on ships, then they're under lockdown inside their quarters, except for the doctor and those of us in here."

The leader paused, his gaze thoughtful. He looked down at the schematic, pointed to the maintenance tunnels, and asked the comm operator, "How many tunnel entry points are there?"

The woman obediently tapped on her screen, and colorful dots appeared, indicating the location of each access hatch.

"You have monitors on those?" he asked.

The woman's eyes darted to her manager, and the man nodded imperceptibly.

"We do. There are sensors on each location."

"Pull up the records."

She did as he asked, and Katie could see the man's shoulders relax as he scanned the data.

He stepped back, waving a hand to his lieutenant. "Stand down. We'll take their word for it." He leveled a glare at the manager. "For now."

Back inside the auxiliary enviro room, Katie blew out a relieved breath. "That was entirely too close."

One good thing had come of this, though. Now that they'd assured themselves the maintenance tunnels were empty, Katie wouldn't have to worry about bumping into anyone as she traversed them—and she planned to do a lot of traversing.

"Y'all ever hear the phrase 'home field advantage'?" she murmured. "Well, suckers, I'm about to go all 'home field' on your ass."

Her fingers danced over the controls as she backed out of the control room, though she kept the console running. Setting it aside, she reached back inside the cubby, and pulled out a bag of particulate colloids.

She would use these to simulate a layer of dust after she left the room. Brownian motion would scatter the colloids for some time; they would move about and then slowly settle onto surfaces, making the room appear unused.

Transferring Fred's magnetic leash to the belt of her EVA suit, she grabbed her console in one hand, and her 'bag of dust' in the other. Shooing Fred out into the tunnel, she took one last look around and then released the colloids.

A second skim coating of ActiveFiber rimmed the door. She activated it, and the material released fine threads that mimicked cobwebs, completing the impression the room had fallen into disuse.

As the door slid shut, she snapped her fingers at the puppy with a small smile. "C'mon, Fred, let's go see Doc."

TEN

SIERRA TWELVE

MAINTENANCE TUNNELS

AS KATIE EXITED the auxiliary room, Team Five was a kilometer away, moving down a perpendicular tunnel toward the central hub. Thad was on point, gliding forward on silent feet, P-SCAR in hand. The rifle's barrel inscribed slow arcs as he advanced to the target. Ell mimicked his actions from the rear as she walked backward, covering their six.

They were headed inward, in search of a network node Jack could use to insinuate himself into the system and spy on those who held Sierra Twelve hostage.

{*Up ahead, on your right, five meters.*} Jack pointed over Thad's shoulder from his position just behind him.

Thad nodded, and his gaze flicked to the feed on his HUD, imagery from the stealth microdrones Jack had unleashed serving as a vanguard.

Everything still read green. The tunnels appeared deserted.

He came to a stop at the bulkhead seam Jack had indicated.

{Looks like you're clear. I'll move on ahead half a klick to the next intersection.}

Jack slipped past with a nod and began working on the panel he needed to remove, to access the node.

Thad used a sticky command to attach one of the microdrones to the tunnel's overhead so he could keep an eye on the intel officer, just in case, and then called back to the team. *{Asha, with me.}*

The medic moved forward, her own P-SCAR in hand, and Thad moved over so that they could walk abreast. Mike hung back with Ell, half a klick in the other direction.

He knew Lane would be standing alongside Jack, waiting to receive the intel officer's data dump. From there, the team lead would decide how they would proceed.

As he and Asha kept watch at the intersection, Thad split his time between monitoring the drones up ahead and the one he'd left behind.

As always, watching Jack in information-gathering mode was a curious thing. The Marine stood in a casual slump, arms crossed and head down, as if in deep contemplation.

Thad knew from past experience that the man was not unaware of his surroundings. Though he might seem oblivious, Jack could snap into a state of readiness faster than anyone Thad had ever seen.

He tensed when he saw Jack do just that.

Lane did the same. *{Campbell?}* Her voice demanded answers.

{Ten in the control center, two patrols, and a trio at the docks.} Jack answered her one-word query in a staccato tone. *{Good news is that we won't have to maintain radio silence on this op. They've blocked all external communications, but the platform residents are free to communicate with each other.}*

{Why'd the hell they allow that?} wondered Mike.

Jack sent a mental shrug. *{Cocky, maybe. Confident that they have this thing sewn up and no one can interfere. With two exceptions, everyone's locked inside their quarters.}*

{What two exceptions?} Lane asked sharply.

{Main control center and Medical, but....}

{But?} Lane prompted.

{Someone else has managed to hack into the system and is spying on the SS, too. They got here before I did.}

{Our intruder?}

Jack nodded. *{That's my best guess. I think I can track him, but I'll need help.}*

Through the drone's camera, Thad saw Lane's eyes narrow thoughtfully.

{Contact the ship and ask Rafe to loan you someone,} she instructed. *{The last thing we need is for some well-intentioned, untrained civvy going vigilante on us.}*

{Copy that. But that's one message I'll have to deliver in person.}

At Lane's lifted brow, the intel officer explained, *{Internal comms are allowed, but external comms are blocked. Scimitar's external.}*

{Go. Find the vigilante and shut him down before he interferes with the op.}

Jack straightened. *{I assume you'll be concentrating on taking out the ones in the control room first?}*

At Lane's 'Yes', an icon appeared on Thad's HUD.

Jack gave a single nod. *{That icon will give you access to the cameras in that room. I'll contact you once our rogue is neutralized.}*

* * *

Back inside *Scimitar,* the flight crew had fallen into a pattern of watchful vigilance, the quiet of the cockpit punctuated only by periodic updates.

Cass's voice cut suddenly into that silence. "Doesn't this bother any of you?"

"Doesn't what bother us?" asked Rafe, not turning from his console.

His disinterest earned a shove to his seat from Cass's boot.

"Some unknown person got here before we did."

Micah saw Cass shoot an annoyed glare at the back of Rafe's

head. *At some point, those two really need to get a room,* he thought privately.

The sexual tension between the captain and the flight engineer was so apparent, even he'd picked up on it, and he'd been told by old girlfriends he wasn't exactly the most observant where things like that were concerned.

"Felt to me like the team just kind of shrugged and went with it," he heard Cass complain. "Don't you want to know who it was, and how in the hell they got here?"

"Sure," agreed Rafe, "but they're in the best position to discover that, not us."

"Not… entirely true," Cass's voice turned sly.

That got the pilot's attention.

Swiveling to pin her with a warning look, Rafe said, "You have a job to do, Chief. Don't go nosing into team business."

The expression on Cass's face was smug. "All I did was tap into the platform's network—like I always do on a mission," she hastily added when his eyes narrowed.

The captain's expression eased, and after a moment's thought, he nodded. "Okay, I'll bite. What did you find?"

She pushed her console's screen to the main holo for them all to see.

"Look here." She gestured, and part of the image lit up. "That's an artificially-introduced bit of RF interference on the band that stations use to host their networks. It's random, but seems to coincide with one of the enviro plants. I did a search, and this is an ongoing problem the platform's had for the past five years. They chalk it up to poorly shielded equipment that Cobalt refuses to replace. Since it's low-intensity, they've pretty much had to live with it, so they ignore it for the most part."

"And you're telling us this because….?"

"Because there's an active band buried in all that interference. And it's awfully coincidental that the frequency of that band is FINGERS."

Rafe's hands stilled. He slid a glance Micah's way and then

turned to face Cass. "That's an old Navy trick," he said slowly.

She grinned. "Thought that'd catch your eye. Still want me to keep my nose out of it, Cap?"

Rafe scraped his palm across the side of his jaw, expression thoughtful. "Jack might connect the dots, since he's a licensed pilot," he mused, "but I doubt anyone else on the team would."

"And his job doesn't call on him to do a whole lot of flying, so it might not be top of mind for him," supplied Micah.

Dana's voice sounded confused. "I don't get it. If someone's already fingered the interference, doesn't that mean they've identified it already?"

Micah shook his head. "Not fingered, as in tagged or IDed it. FINGERS is a frequency pilots use to communicate with each other." He held up his hand, folding a finger down as he reeled off the numbers. "One, two, three… four, five."

He nodded toward the front screen, where Cass had pulled up the EHF 123.45 frequency label, and Dana's expression cleared.

"That suggests we're dealing with a pilot, then."

Cass nodded. "It fits. And it's got to be someone local to the platform. My cred's on whoever's running the gray market here."

Rafe's brows rose. "You think so?"

Cass scoffed. "Aw, c'mon, Cap. You know as well as I do that there's always a market for hard-to-get, low-risk stuff that everyone wants but can't obtain legally. A copy of the latest bootlegged tri-D release. Maybe some premium liquor or stim sticks, without paying duty taxes. Betcha the pilot's set up FINGERS as a listening post, a way he can pick up instructions from this contact."

Rafe shot her a knowing look. "Figured that out awfully quick, didn't you? Almost like you have experience with it yourself."

Cass smacked her hand against her chest, her face the picture of innocence. "I'm wounded, Cap. Truly." Nodding to the display, she added, "I just keep my ear to the ground, is all—and my nose clean."

Micah's cough hid a laugh, and if Cass's glare was any indication, he would have received a boot to the back of his cradle if he'd been in reach.

"Regardless," she continued, turning back to Rafe to press her point, "don't you think it's worth looking into? I've traced the origin of the signal. It's not too far from the hatch."

Rafe rubbed at his chin once more, his eyes resting thoughtfully on Cass. Abruptly, he nodded.

"Okay, it's worth checking out." He looked over at Micah. "You go. I'll man the drones—"

"Hold up," Cass called out. "Someone's at the hatch."

Micah heard a rustling sound and looked back to see Dana had taken a knee, her P-SCAR rifle in hand, trained on the open umbilical.

An IFF ping appeared on the ship's overlay, identifying the intruder as Jack.

The Marine's head appeared in the hatch. "Need your help. Lane's decided we need to corral our unknown before he interferes with the op."

Micah looked over at Rafe, who nodded. Unwebbing from his co-pilot's cradle, he brushed past Dana and headed aft.

Jack nodded and retreated back into the airlock.

ELEVEN

KATIE HAD PLENTY of time to think and remember as she made the five-kilometer trek to Medical.

On the rare occasions she could get Doc Slater to talk about his time in the Navy, he'd shared with her some of the things he'd learned. She pulled up a conversation in her memory now.

"If you ever find yourself in a life-or-death situation, remember the OODA Loop." Slater's voice rang in her head, his words as clear as if he was walking alongside her. *"Observe. Orient. Decide. Act. These steps may save your life one day."*

Katie blinked rapidly as she turned the concept over in her head.

"Observation is vital in decision-making. What affects you immediately? What could impact you later on?"

"Observe. Okay, I've done some of that already," she murmured softly. "Ten people in the control center. Let's see where else they are…."

She walked through the various feeds using the console she

carried, looking for other incursions. She found two roaming pairs, and a trio standing guard at the dock, but no others.

Her eyes narrowed in thought as her mentor's voice continued to play in her head.

"Orient. Learn to recognize the barriers that interfere with your goal. This gives you an edge over your opponent."

She returned her attention to the control center, flipping between various angles. She took note of the number and type of weapons, and tried to identify weaknesses she could exploit.

None immediately came to mind, and her frustration grew as she came up with and discarded a few different ideas.

Anything she could think to do to incapacitate the intruders would equally harm her own people.

At least the Cobalt employees' overall condition seemed stable. A few appeared to be favoring injured limbs, and Jeremy sported a black eye and a busted lip, but that was about it.

Lockdown had been initiated platform-wide. That was good; it meant most of the six thousand workers and their family members were safely tucked away in their personal quarters. The public spaces were now fair game for any plan she could think to implement.

She decided to focus first on those who weren't inside the control room. She'd whittle down their numbers, wage a war of attrition before tackling the main group.

Medical was just ahead, down a branching passageway. As she neared, Katie accessed the security holorecorder mounted just above the doorway.

The image resolved on the console's 2-D screen, and she saw Doc was not alone; a patient lay on one of the diagnostic beds. Slater was leaning over the man, examining him. Additionally, a woman stood guard at the entrance, her weapon trained on them.

Doc was being very deliberate with his movements, and explaining everything he was about to do before he did it. Katie realized he was doing this to make sure the woman would find no reason to discharge the weapon she held.

"I don't need a play-by-play, Doc," the woman sneered. "Just get this idiot patched up so I can get you both back in lockdown. No one's allowed outside their quarters; no exceptions."

Katie studied the injured man, trying to identify which Cobalt employee had been hurt, but Doc was blocking him. When he shifted far enough to reveal the patient's face, Katie nearly groaned aloud.

Why did it have to be Old Jerry?

The guy was the biggest gossip she knew; he couldn't keep a secret to save his soul. There was no help for it. She'd just have to wait him out.

She moved to the maintenance closet that provided service access to Medical's equipment, jimmied the lock, and opened the door. Fred darted inside, and she followed after, sealing the door shut behind her. She leaned her console against a nearby wall and then turned to study her surroundings.

The closet was long and narrow, with barely enough room for her to maneuver. To her right, modules lined the inner wall, each unit powering one of the heavy diagnostic beds in the main bay. To her left was the platform's lone surgical unit. A large panel, almost as tall as she was, provided access to the back of the machine.

She'd watched Doc make an adjustment to the device once from the front side, and knew its interior was roomy enough for Fred to squeeze through. Once Old Jerry left, she'd hand the pup over and be on her way.

On second thought…

Katie frowned as it occurred to her that the doctor might try and stop her from doing something he considered foolish.

Sometimes he still sees me as the kid he was saddled with when my dad was killed.

As quietly as she could, she began working the screws loose on the back of the surgical unit. When she had the last one undone, she lifted the panel clear of the unit and set it aside gently, being careful not to make any noise.

She'd wait until Old Jerry left, lift Fred through to the other side, and then scoot back out before Doc had a chance to stop her.

Fred had other ideas. Eager to see one of his favorite humans, the basset puppy whined, scratching against the plating.

Katie spun around, grabbed his paw, and shook her head sternly. "No," she whispered.

Fred responded with a loud, deep *woof* that reverberated through the small closet and off the metal sides of the surgical unit.

"*Shit!*" Katie hissed, her eyes flying to the console's 2-D screen. She saw the woman holding the gun whip her head around in the direction of the surgical suite.

"What was that? I thought you said you were alone in here." The woman's voice was threaded with suspicion.

Old Jerry lifted his head and looked blearily around. "Sounded like Fred, but it can't be. Katie was out hauling ore today."

Doc's hand jerked in reaction to Old Jerry's words, and the grizzled dockhand shot the doctor an apologetic look. Katie realized at that moment that the news of *Goblin*'s demise must have reached him.

"Sorry for your loss, Doc," muttered Jerry with an awkward pat of his hand.

"Who's Fred?" the woman demanded, stepping toward them.

Katie saw Slater's eyes dart up to the security feed, and then over toward the surgical suite. "Fred's my foster daughter's dog."

"I thought she always took Fred with her when she flew," Old Jerry protested.

Katie wanted to smack him for that. *Just... keep your mouth **shut**, Jerry.*

"Not this time," the doctor replied, looking up once more at the security holorecorder.

That was the second time he'd done that. The expression in his eyes made Katie realize he suspected she was alive, and that she'd hacked into the system.

It was no great stretch; he'd caught her doing it enough as a teen.

"I didn't see no dog when I searched the place," the woman interposed, suspicion morphing into skepticism.

"That's because he was sleeping under my office desk." Annoyance edged Doc's voice. "Obviously, he's awake now."

The intruder grunted and stepped sideways toward Doc's office, her pistol still pointed at the two men.

The movement galvanized Katie into action.

She reached through to the front of the surgical unit and slid the catch that held the panel closed. Hauling Fred up into her arms, she whispered, "Go on. Go to Doc." Pushing carefully past the tangle of wiring, she set him down inside the room.

The basset puppy turned to look over his shoulder, as if asking, *"Aren't you coming?"*

Katie nudged him further into the room—not an easy task, as Fred had decided to plant his butt on the floor, and she was as far out as she could be without toppling over. She managed to shove him clear and close the unit just as footsteps approached from the hallway outside.

She could just make out Doc's muffled voice. "Fred, you awake now, little guy? You know you're supposed to stay in my office. Come on out of there, now."

The patter of clawed feet reached her ears as Fred responded to Doc's call and trotted toward him.

She heard Doc pause and whisper, "Be careful, Katie-girl," before he retreated back to the main bay, dog in tow.

A pang of regret hit her. "I'll be back as soon as I can," she promised on a whisper of her own, although he couldn't hear. "I just have a few things to do first."

Katie pulled herself free and set the unit's back panel into place, her fingers swiftly spinning the screws' threads until they were secure. That done, she scooped up her console and prepared to slip back out into the maintenance tunnels.

As she turned for the door, her eyes landed on a pile of discarded shock-locks. There were six in all, each thirty centimeters in length. They'd originally been used to secure the three diagnostic modules hanging on the wall, inside of which rested three extremely expensive AdS/CFT computer cores.

The locks were the very best the industry had to offer. They functioned as active deterrents, rendering the units tamper-proof to all but licensed repair service bots.

Unfortunately, one of the many problems that plagued doctors who worked on remote platforms such as this one was the lack of access to such repair bots.

The manufacturer had reluctantly agreed to forward a service manual so that Doc could upgrade the cores himself. Katie had been with him that day, and had witnessed firsthand the kind of electric shock those locks would deliver to someone who tinkered with them without the proper codes. After that, Doc had decided it was more trouble than it was worth to reinstall them, and they'd lain there in a discarded pile ever since.

The third and fourth steps of the OODA Loop nudged at the back of her brain: *Decide. Act.*

She bent and scooped them up, fingering the label she'd attached to the bundle years ago, where the access codes that would reactivate them was written in her own messy scrawl. Looping them over one shoulder, she stepped out into the tunnel, shut the door behind her, and set out in search of the roaming patrols.

TWELVE

SIERRA TWELVE
MAINTENANCE TUNNELS

"THE RF INTERFERENCE signal is coming from up there." Jack pointed down the tunnel as Micah emerged from the airlock.

An icon flashed on Micah's HUD, and when he accessed it, a map popped up, indicating some sort of maintenance room up ahead.

He glanced at the identifying tag. "Auxiliary environmental?"

Jack nodded. "That's what it says."

"That's the origin of the frequency buried in there, too? FINGERS?"

Jack pulled to a stop just in front of the door and placed his hand on the palmpad. He shot Micah a sidelong look. "You noticed that, too?"

"Yeah. Well, Cass did. She pointed it out to us." Micah nodded to the door. "Locked?"

"Not for long."

After a few seconds, the door slid open under the intelligence officer's hand, revealing cobwebs undulating gently in the slight breeze the door's movement had generated. Jack reached out, wrapping his fingers around the delicate threads.

"Looks like no one's been here in a while," commented Micah, but Jack shook his head, bending forward to examine the cobweb more closely.

"Actually, I'm not sure that's the case." His tone was thoughtful.

He pushed past the web lining the entrance and palmed the lights on. As he pulled back, he traced the edge of the doorframe with his hand, a curious expression in his eyes.

"Well, I'll be damned," he said softly. A slow grin spread across his face, but he didn't say anything else.

"Hey, jarhead. Hanging in suspense over here," Micah reminded him.

Jack elbowed him. "Chill, Navy. This kind of genius deserves respect."

Micah leaned against the doorjamb and crossed his arms. "Genius? Respect?"

"Whoever we're dealing with, they're pretty clever. This is some devious shit." Jack returned his attention to the delicate threads blocking the door. "When I felt the strands, they didn't have the texture a real spider's web would. Although most people would probably dismiss it, just like you did—no insult intended," he added as an afterthought.

Micah snorted. "Sure there was. Jarhead."

Ignoring the jibe, Jack tapped on the edge of the doorframe. "There's a very narrow band of ActiveFiber material lining this. What you're seeing was formed from that."

"No shit?" Micah leaned forward to get a better look. "That's pretty convincing."

Jack nodded. "Yep. And ActiveFiber could spin out something like this in a matter of minutes."

Micah looked beyond the threshold and into the room. "Which means that layer of dust we're seeing on everything is probably fake too."

"Yeah," Jack said. "I'd bet good credits on it."

"Any idea who it is?"

Jack shook his head. "No, but if this is the same person who hacked the external hatch, it must be a platform native. No one from the SS would be familiar enough with the area. They wouldn't have had the time to set up a program this elaborate to run the ActiveFiber, either."

"So we have a Cobalt employee on the loose, waging their own war against a bunch of terrorists… Is that what you're telling me?"

Jack shot him a worried look. "That's exactly what I'm saying." He swept the fake cobwebs out of the way, stepped into the room, and pointed. "The RF's coming from behind that wall, by the way."

He crossed the room and laid his palms flat against a section of wall. To Micah's surprise, it rolled back, exposing a hidden access panel.

"More ActiveFiber?"

"Got it in one." Jack opened the panel and stuck his head inside. His voice echoed slightly from within. "Yeah, that's what I thought. This is where the leaf node is."

"Want to break that down for us dumb Navy pilots?"

Jack pulled his head back. "Leaf node's the end of the line, so to speak. It's the very last computer node in a sequence. It's also where our hacker tapped into the public net." His expression was distant, his voice distracted.

Micah realized the intelligence man must have dropped some sort of hack onto the node so that he could contact-trace their mysterious web-spinning, free-range local.

A wry grin crossed Jack's face. "The work's a bit messy, but the code's solid. Whoever he is, this kid—and yes, I do think it's a kid—has promise."

His grin widened at Micah's look of confusion. "Most platforms have a small group of kids, employees' children, who are raised there," he explained. "Platform rats are easily bored, stuck on a small station like this for long periods of time. They can get into an interesting amount of trouble when left on their own."

"You speaking from personal experience, there?" Micah lifted a brow.

"Might've done something like this myself, once upon a time, but you'll never get me to admit to it." He resealed the access panel, letting the ActiveFiber skim coating hide it from view once more.

Stepping back toward the entrance, Jack swept his gaze across the contents of the room. "Now all we have to do is figure out whose kid is out there trying to get himself killed."

"And you think you'll be able to locate our super sleuth by that tap you dropped on them?"

Jack's eyes glinted with a dark humor. "Oh ye of little faith. Of course I will." He hooked a thumb in the direction of the hub as they exited back out into the tunnel. "Our culprit's thataway."

Micah fell into step beside Jack as the Marine started down the tunnel passage at a brisk walk.

"Any chance those SS jokers will find our guy before we do?" the pilot asked.

Jack's face turned momentarily grim. "Let's hope not. Even if this kid's as clever as I think, he's no match for them. His willingness to take them on concerns me."

Micah glanced over at him. "In what way?"

Jack frowned. "If they're willing to shoot at an unshielded and unarmed ship like that tug they took out, then they'll think nothing of taking out someone who tries to cross them. Honestly," he gave a small shrug, "I don't think the lives of these miners mean all that much to them, other than as a means to an end."

They fell into a combat-ready silence, Jack intent upon his trace, and Micah monitoring the passageway up ahead with a small cloud of stealthed microdrones he'd brought along.

"Ahhh," Jack breathed after a moment, breaking the silence. "Our genius is a *she*."

* * *

One of the pairs of patrolling intruders was about to swing into a section of the platform known for its sporadic systems failures. It was low on the repair list, given that it was located in a little-used area, reserved for overflow in the warehouse section.

"Let's see if we can't figure out a way to neutralize you guys, what d'ya say?" Katie murmured as she reviewed what she had to work with in this sector.

She grinned to herself as an idea came to her. It would take some time to set up, but it was a simple plan, really.

First, isolate a single HVAC zone in that sector, and send its ambient temperature plunging to well below the freezing point. Second, drop the temperature of the water line feeding the backup fire sprinklers that ran through the area until it hovered just above the freezing point.

She glanced at her chrono. It would take time for the temperature to drop low enough to enact her plan. She'd have to wait until the intruders made their next pass to fully implement it.

After they passed through that sector, and the section had enough time to bleed off residual heat, it would be time for part three of the plan: set the sprinklers to release a fine spray of supercooled water. Wherever the water landed, the surface would flash freeze on contact.

If she played her cards right, the thin coating would barely be seen. Plus, she was banking on the intruders being too distracted by the subarctic temperatures to notice anything else.

Katie inserted a time-delayed, motion-activated program that would kick in right before the patrol hit that section again. She planned everything carefully, programming the system to check in with her before each decision point. By her estimation, she had about an hour to commandeer a weapon and position herself to take out the two as they entered the icy corridor.

Piece of cake.

Having set the trap to her satisfaction, Katie moved onto the next pair of intruders prowling the platform.

The path these walked would take them close by one of the tunnel entrances just ahead. She studied her prey, following them as they drew closer, transiting from one sensor pickup to the next. She smothered a laugh as one of the invaders nearly smacked into the door that led into the next sector.

That door sensor is always on the fritz. Gage claims it keeps shorting out on him—

Katie's hand froze over the display as she realized what she'd just been thinking.

"Shorted out…." she breathed, her fingers flying over her console's ancient keyboard as she searched for the platform's automated access control system. "*Aha.* Gotcha."

Her connection to the building's service portal would gain her admittance. She copied the settings from the glitchy door over to the one the pair was approaching, and waited to see what would happen. She gave a mental whoop, shoving her fist in the air when, just as before, the door's sensors didn't trigger an automatic opening.

"Seriously?" she heard one of them say.

The other man kicked at the door. "What a piece of shit platform."

You keep telling yourselves that, Katie said to herself with a gleeful cackle as she accessed the doors between where they were and where she stood waiting for them.

Every door would now require a physical palm to activate. They weren't coded to any particular print; the metal plate simply required a human palm to complete the circuit. At last she could begin staging her trap.

Diving into the controls to the palmpad on the final door, she increased the voltage running through it, bypassing the built-in safety protocols.

This last door wouldn't just not open for them; it would deliver a powerful electrical shock to the person whose palm made contact with the surface of that metal plate. If she got really lucky, the second man would brush up against the first, and she'd be able to neutralize both at the same time.

"Don't count on it, Katie," she muttered to herself. "Remember what Doc always says: 'Luck is the residue of preparation.' Icing on the cake, nothing more."

She was still uncertain how to keep them from contacting their associates once she captured them. The best she could come up with was to increase the RF interference in this section, but it would cut her off from the public net, too. She'd be blind until she retreated far enough to regain signal.

She straightened as the far doors slid open to admit her targets. Apparently they'd resigned themselves to the need to use the palmpads to access the next section of passageway. As they strode toward the door, they gave no indication they suspected foul play, though their disgust with Sierra Twelve was clear.

She set her console down on the ground, dumping all but four of the shock-locks into a pile beside it. Katie would use the four she still held to bind the pair of intruders, one each for hands and feet.

She stood poised to open the tunnel door, her body vibrating with tension. A look of pure anticipation formed on her face as one man slapped his palm down on the surface of the display.

She heard a garbled sound fly from his lips, and then his body grew rigid.

"What the fu—" his companion started to say, rounding on him impatiently, a hand sweeping out to grab at the frozen man's arm.

With a yelp, the second man jumped back, realizing in the nick of time what was happening.

"Oh shit, oh shit, oh shit," he chanted, looking around for anything nonconducting that he could use to knock his partner free.

Finding nothing, the man let out a growling yell and charged, his momentum carrying both free of the panel, although Katie knew it still must have imparted a sharp sting in the process.

As she watched, the second man groaned and rolled onto his back, his expression contorted in pain.

That was Katie's cue to move.

She burst from her hiding place with an exclamation of stunned surprise. "Omigosh, are you okay?"

She feigned concern as she stepped past the second man and

knelt beside the one who'd received the electric shock. Rolling him to his side, she pretended to look for wounds while reaching for his weapon.

"Back off, bitch," she heard the other man growl.

Her eyes widened as she looked up and saw him reaching for his weapon, just as her own hand wrapped around the handle of the first man's pistol.

With no time to check the weapon's settings, she aimed it at the second man and pulled the trigger.

THIRTEEN

Sierra Twelve
Maintenance tunnels

"Sonofa—!" Jack broke into a sprint.

Micah didn't bother to ask; he just followed as the other man went barreling down the tunnel passage.

The intelligence officer swerved suddenly, taking a hard left down a cross corridor. Micah did the same, his hand slapping against the bulkhead's surface to redirect his momentum as he went.

{What just happened?}

{Fool girl just took out one of the patrols, but she didn't block their communications first. Those jackasses in control know she's on the loose.}

Micah turned Jack's words over in his head as the Marine increased his speed.

{That doesn't sound like something your whiz kid would miss.}

*{Oh, she tried. She thought increasing the interference in that area would do the trick. It almost worked. But the fact that it's concentrated **only** at the spot—}*

Micah abruptly understood. *{That's a dead giveaway.}*

{Yeah,} agreed Jack. *{She's not used to thinking things through tactically. I let the RF interference ride, since she's already outed herself, but we need to secure those two before someone is sent to retrieve them, and undoes all her work.}*

Jack pulled to a stop in front of a closed access door, lifting a fisted hand in silent warning. *{Let me confirm the cameras are off.}*

After a beat, he nodded. Sliding the door open far enough to launch a surveillance microdrone, Jack brought his weapon up into its ready position and palmed the door.

It slid open to reveal two slumped figures. One was cuffed; the other was not.

{Where's the girl?} asked Micah.

{Running scared, probably. I'm surprised we didn't bump into her on our way here.} Jack stopped in front of the unsecured man, took a knee, and felt for a pulse. *{Dead. The other?}* he jerked his chin to indicate the man Micah knelt beside.

{Tagged and bagged. Don't ask me what she used to secure him; I've never seen it before, and it just gave me a helluva shock when I brushed my fingers against it.}

Jack bent down to inspect the device. *{Huh. Never seen one of those used to cuff a guy.}*

{What is it?}

Jack stood, hefting the dead body. *{Shock-lock. Used to keep meddling thieves from stealing mainframe cores. Avoid touching it and you'll be fine.}*

{Easy for you to say,} Micah grumbled, but he hooked his hands under the man's armpits and dragged him into the tunnels.

Jack indicated a supply closet up ahead, and they dumped both bodies inside.

Micah stepped back, staring down at the two SS men. *{Any idea how she did it?}*

Jack chuckled audibly. *{Yeah. She disabled automatic access control, and forced them to use the palmpad to open the doors. Then she bypassed the pad's safeties and shocked the hell out of the one you carried. I'm no medic, but from the looks of it, she followed it with a* *point-blank directed energy shot. He'll be out for a while.}*

Micah indicated the dead body. *{And this guy?}*

Jack shook his head. *{No idea. Likely the weapon she stole was set to deliver a killing strike. I'm guessing she either didn't know, or didn't have the time to check before having to defend herself. Either way, I'd be willing to bet it's her first time.}*

{That's going to have a profound effect on her.}

{ No shit, Navy.} Jack shot him a grim look. *{Another reason we need to find her, and fast.}*

* * *

The team was huddled in the shadows just outside the control center when Jack sent them an update. His mental voice cut into their review of the center's ingress points.

The news was met with various levels of surprise.

{She took them out all on her own?} Mike's voice was tinged with surprise and a grudging respect.

{Not without some cost,} cautioned Jack. *{I estimate we have five minutes, maybe ten, before those goons in control realize their patrol hasn't reported in. Be ready; they're not going to let that ride.}*

Thad glanced around at the rest of the team. His HUD's IFF painted each figure with a bright green outline as his drakeskin suit's predictive system identified them as 'Friend' and not 'Foe.'

Lane's outline motioned to the team sniper. *{Ell, you're here.}*

A pin dropped onto the diagram currently displayed over the combat net, landing on the control center's downspin wall. On the other side was an empty conference room.

{Return air vent, shared by both spaces,} Lane explained. *{It should give you coverage of two-thirds of the room. Go.}*

Ell's shadowed form nodded, and the sniper glided silently away.

Next, Lane pointed to the area beneath a bank of consoles facing the door. *{Asha, you're smallest. You come in from here.}*

Thad caught Asha's brief hesitation before she nodded.

Being the smallest often meant crawling through narrow spaces and cramming herself into tight spots. This time, it meant sliding between subflooring until she came to the underside of the console. Asha would have to wedge herself between bundles of wiring in order to fit into the spot, but it was the only way to cover that side of the control center, opposite the door.

The big Marine could only imagine how much fun those assignments were.

As Asha moved into position, Lane turned to Mike. *{You're on overwatch. Set up half a klick back the way we came, and let us know if anyone approaches.}*

{Copy that, ma'am.}

As the demolition expert strode back down the concourse, Lane motioned Thad toward the control center's entrance. They took up station on either side of the door and waited for the others to get into position.

* * *

Katie's hands shook. Hell, her whole body shook. She recognized it for what it was: a delayed response to the action she'd just taken.

The situation had begun to take on the air of a challenge, almost a game. But it had suddenly become all too real.

She'd just killed a man, point-blank.

"Oh crap. Oh crap," she chanted softly.

She sucked in a deep breath and forcibly shoved the mental image of the man's body from her mind. She understood that she was compartmentalizing, and knew she'd have a reckoning later, but she needed to focus.

She fell back on the mental discipline that had been drilled into her as a pilot. There was risk in every flight. The very medium through which she piloted each vessel was one utterly inhospitable to human life. When things went wrong, it wasn't like she could pull over and get out. She had to deal with her current state head-on and find a way through it to the other side.

Aviate. Navigate. Communicate.

The pilot's mantra that had been drilled into her saved her sanity now. She would concentrate on stabilizing her situation, do what she could to eliminate the remainder of the intruders, and then figure out a way to call for help. In that order.

She forced herself to move on to her next destination, the central loading dock at the end of the east spar. As she did, she mentally reviewed the materials that were available to her there.

It was an area she knew well, having spent months in the mechanics bay during her ground school lessons, learning the ins and outs of the ships she would pilot before she flew them. The S&Ps—the spaceframe and powerplant engineers who maintained the ships—had been willing teachers when they realized how eagerly Katie soaked up all the knowledge they had to give.

She'd spent many an hour packing slippery, greasy ball bearings into rings. She knew better than most what a hazard they could be if stepped on. Two years earlier, she'd twisted an ankle on one, fallen, and chipped her elbow. Doc had mended it, but not before Mack, her S&P instructor, had chewed her out for her carelessness.

She smiled down at the huge canisters of ball bearings as she recalled his words: *"Don't leave shit scattered around. You leave it out, some fool's gonna trip over it."*

Oh yeah, she thought. *These'll make a fine trap.* And she could use herself as the bait.

The dock was eerily quiet, with only the three strangers standing guard. Katie kept to the shadows, her back pressed against the bulkheads as she eased her way deeper into the area.

The door to the mechanics room was open and unlocked, left that way by the three goons after they'd rounded up all the Cobalt employees. Katie forced herself not to wonder about the workers who'd been here when the ship docked so unexpectedly.

She also kept her eyes averted, ignoring the dark stain marring the open expanse of deck—something she strongly suspected might be blood. Instead, she focused her attention on the three men standing guard as she slipped into the bay, her shoulders relaxing somewhat when she made it there without incident.

The room was lit by nothing more than emergency lights, which suited Katie just fine. Moving with silent confidence, she angled her way to the shelves lining the far wall, where stacks of parts were stored.

As she neared, her eyes caught on her objective: boxes filled with ball bearings, almost too heavy for her to lift on her own.

Pulling a maglev cart away from its charging port against an adjacent wall, she carefully set three full boxes onto the cart. These were followed by two canisters of lubricating grease.

She pushed the cart over to a side exit, wedging her fingers into the seam of the doors to ease them apart manually. She held her breath as she pushed the cart out into the shadowed recesses of the dock. Her destination, the entrance off the main corridor, was a mere twenty meters away.

The focus of the three men remained outward, toward the bay doors and the external sensor feed that showed any approaching vessels. Their backs were to the door, confident as they were in the knowledge that they had every Cobalt person locked away in their quarters.

Still, staging her trap in full sight of the three men was more than Katie was willing to risk. She opted for the smaller, secondary door instead. It was off to the side, and out of their line of sight.

There was a catwalk that wrapped around the dock, lining three of the four bulkheads. Conveniently, there was a ladder—well, more a wall of rungs, built into the bulkhead just to the right of the door— that led up to it.

Katie grabbed a length of steel cable and slung it over one shoulder. She lifted one of the boxes of ball bearings, hefting it carefully up each rung as she climbed. The box was heavy, so it was a slow, tedious process, but her tall, rangy body was deceptively strong, toned by months of hard work on Cobalt tugs.

Once on the catwalk, she carefully positioned the box right at the walkway's edge, just above the door. Looping the steel cable around the container, she threaded it across two ceiling joists before coiling the rest into a bundle that dangled within arm's reach from the floor.

She climbed back down and took stock of the items remaining on her cart. Before she could scatter the ball bearings, she needed to fully coat them, both to minimize any noise they might make, and to increase the hazard of the trap.

Opening the first can of grease, she dumped great globs of the thick sludge into the remaining two boxes of ball bearings, working it with her hands to evenly coat them. She took her time, pausing when there was a lull in the conversation between the thugs, only to resume when they began talking once more.

It felt to Katie like it took forever to quietly upend the two boxes and get the small, round, goopy spheres in place, but finally, she was done. She stood back, surveying her work with a sliver of satisfaction.

Now all she had to do was bait them into chasing after her. Her course was committed to memory—a narrow corridor free of both axle grease and ball bearings.

All she had to do was piss them off enough that they'd abandon their posts to hunt her down.

Guess it's showtime....

FOURTEEN

SIERRA TWELVE
MAIN CONCOURSE

{*HEADS UP,*} MIKE called out from his position farther down the concourse. {*Incoming. Looks like one tango, one hostage. Hostage appears to be injured.*}

Thad and Lane backed away from the door, their weapons tracking the two figures as they approached.

{*Can you see any change from inside?*} Lane asked Ell.

The sniper was quiet for a beat, and then said, {*No.*}

Thad scanned the approaching figures with a trained eye. The way the tango moved suggested she had no real military training. By this point, the team had come to the conclusion that none of the secessionists did.

His gaze shifted over to the older man the woman was shepherding. He held his side as if injured, and was sporting a slight limp.

"Move it," he heard the woman snap. She punctuated her words with a small shove.

Thad's jaw worked, and he forcibly tamped down on the anger that rose at the sight.

The man stumbled, recovered, and then shot the armed intruder a heated glare. "Moving as fast as these old bones will carry me, you secessionist bitch," he snarled.

When she moved to shove him again, he flinched away, and picked up his pace.

*{I'd like to shove **her**,}* said Mike, his tone one of quiet rage.

{Copy that,} Thad murmured. *{Stay chill, hoss. Stay chill.}*

{Get ready,} Lane warned. *{We go in when they go in.}*

Following her cue, Thad released a small cloud of audio chaff and then activated the magnetic field that would keep the colloid cloud close around him. He stood poised, his posture mirroring Lane's, two unseen warriors ready to spring into action.

The woman must have contacted the team inside the control center over a private channel, for as she and her prisoner approached, Thad could hear muffled shouts being exchanged from within. He could tell something had the leader agitated, but the feed Jack had hacked wasn't great at separating out voices, and the SS members were talking over one another, exchanging heated words that came out in garbled yells.

{Sounds to me like they think someone has managed to escape confinement,} Lane commented after a moment.

{No, it's not that. I think…} Asha paused.

From her vantage point under the consoles, she could hear the clearest, so they waited for her to fill them in.

{They know about the vigilante,} she finally announced. *{They discovered her when they couldn't reach the patrol she took out. The woman coming your way claims that old man can tell them who it is. Something about a guy named Fred. No, hold on.}* Asha's voice sounded confused. *{A…**dog** named Fred?}*

Over the feed, Thad saw the young man sitting at the traffic controller's console blanch at those words. His hand jerked, knocking a stylus to the ground.

{That didn't go unnoticed,} Lane observed.

One of the SS men, their leader, stalked toward the young man.

{He's demanding that Jeremy tell them more about Fred and his owner,} Asha supplied. *{Jeremy's saying something about the dog usually accompanying its owner on her flights, but not this time.}*

As the woman and her prisoner neared, the control center's doors parted. Thad slipped through, followed by Lane. They took up stations on either side of the door just as the old man limped across the threshold. Everyone inside stopped talking and turned to look expectantly at the newcomers.

"Well?" the SS leader demanded.

The woman who had brought the old man in gestured for him to speak. "Tell 'em."

"Ain't nothing to tell." The old man scowled.

"That dog wasn't there when we got to Medical, and now it is. Where's its owner?"

Thad saw the old man's eyes land on the young man at the STC console. Something passed between the two.

"You kilt her, ya secessionist bastards," the old man said, his voice starting out soft, only to rise at the end as his ire built. "She was the one on that tug, an' ye blew her outa the black!"

{Our vigilante's the pilot of that tug?} asked Ell.

{It fits,} Lane's mental tone was thoughtful.

Thad's eyes landed on Lane's outline. *{Guess I'd assumed our hacker was someone closer in, a dockworker maybe, or someone working an EVA repair.}*

She shifted, her head turning as if to look at him. He saw her nod. *{I'm sure that's what she was banking on. Who would have thought she'd launch herself from a tug a few hundred thousand klicks out?}*

{Look at the Cobalt employees' faces; they've come to the same conclusion. The STC controller's trying to hide it, but he's a poor actor,} Ell commented.

"Get back down there," Thad heard the secessionist leader order the woman who had brought the old man in. He gestured to one of his men. "Gardner, go with her. I want that doctor—and the dog—rounded up."

Thad glanced over at Lane, wondering how she would handle the tangos splitting up and potentially taking more hostages. He saw her arm rise, the silhouette warning him to stay his hand as the two SS thugs passed by his position on their way out the door.

{Mike, two tangos coming your way. En route to Medical. Follow and neutralize.}

{Good copy. Will follow and neutralize,} came Mike's voice. It returned after a moment's pause. *{Boss? You see what Jack just sent?}*

Thad's gaze flicked down to the lower left of his HUD, where an icon blinked at him. Its tag read *'our vigilante.'* Toggling it brought up a personnel file, a smiling photo of a tall, gangly young woman, proudly holding a puppy.

Katie Hyer. Age: 18. Orphaned, age 12. Recently emancipated.
Foster father: James Slater. Chief Medical Officer, Sierra Twelve.

{Shit, she's just a kid.}

{A year past minimum recruitment age,} Lane reminded him.

{Old enough to have skills; young enough to have no sense of her own mortality,} Ell's voice slid into the silence.

Another icon blinked, this time a report from Jack. Thad brought it up alongside the other, and skimmed it quickly.

{Jack thinks he may have found her. They're on their way to intercept.}

* * *

Micah glanced over at Jack as they closed in on their vigilante. *{Hard to believe the person who took out those two secessionists is an eighteen-year-old. That's one hell of an EVA she did.}*

{She did it with a disabled locator beacon, too. Kid's got balls, you gotta give her that.} The look on Jack's face was one of grudging admiration.

They'd just crossed behind the central hub when Jack stopped abruptly, one hand raised in warning.

Micah brought the reticle of his CUSP to his eye, but the other man waved it down.

{Not us. Her.}

{That's a bit vague, Jack. Care to explain?}

Jack gave a low chuckle. *{I'm monitoring her activities. Take a look. In this instance, I think a picture really is worth a thousand words.}*

A feed popped up on Micah's overlay, labeled with the tag, *'Sierra Twelve Warehouse, Sector Delta-Four.'*

Something about the image seemed out of place, but he couldn't quite put his finger on it. Then it hit him.

Most civilian stations and platforms had an edge of grunge to them, especially in less trafficked areas, like a warehouse sector. But this one had a sheen to it. It was shiny, spit-polished like a Navy deck after a staff sergeant ordered his new recruits to clean it.

Seconds later, Micah realized why, when the door slid open to admit a man and a woman. Both were armed, identifying them as one of the SS patrols. The minute their feet hit the warehouse floor, the secessionists went sprawling, and their weapons spun away.

{It's covered in ice!}

The sprinkler system must have been tied into the sector's sensors, because the instant motion was detected, they came online. Based on the intruders' shouts, the water was also super-chilled.

Jack brought up the sensor data streaming from the warehouse. *{Take a look at that temperature.}*

It was well below the freezing point.

{Clever,} said Micah. *{I'd be willing to bet those guns are now flash-frozen to the floor.}*

{If they aren't now, they will be soon,} the intel officer agreed.

The sprinklers shut off, and a sticky, red foam descended. Micah knew from experience that the nano-laced fire suppressant would cling persistently to every surface it landed on, human and weapon alike.

{See what I mean? We can't underestimate this kid—} Jack cut off abruptly, a look of consternation on his face. It quickly morphed

into anger as he let out a low curse. *{Fool girl's determined to get herself killed!}*

He broke into a sprint, and Micah followed.

{Now what?}

{Just got a blip on her. She's at the dock.}

Micah's brows climbed into his hairline. *{She's got to suspect by now that they're onto her. You think she's still going to try something?}*

Jack's silhouette twitched, and Micah knew if they weren't stealthed, he'd have been treated to an incredulous glance.

*{She just took out two roving patrols. What the hell do **you** think? The dock's the only other place, outside the control center, where these goons are stationed.}*

His tone turned speculative. *{I'm sure she already has a plan. We just need to reach her before she implements it, or be there to support her when things go sideways.}* He slowed as they approached the dock, moving to one side of the tunnel as he crept slowly forward.

They still had another ten meters to go when things erupted.

* * *

{Katie Hyer.}

The voice that sounded over the platform's public net was the same one that had taken Jeremy's place on the STC channel.

The fact it was calling her by name brought Katie to a stop, one hand resting on the back of the man she'd just secured with her last remaining shock-lock.

{Katie Hyer,} the voice repeated. *{We know you're out there, and we know what you're doing. We have your dog and your foster father. Turn yourself in now, or they both die.}*

FIFTEEN

Sierra Twelve

Maintenance tunnels

{*WELL, SHIT.*} JACK'S voice sounded disgusted. *{So much for the subtle approach.}*

In the next instant, he reappeared beside Micah, his drakeskin's stealth disabled. He motioned Micah forward.

"She had to have heard that. It was piped throughout the platform," Micah said.

Jack nodded and then jerked his chin down the tunnel passage. "Dock's another fifteen meters, just around that curve. We'll need to be careful," he warned in a low tone. "She's armed, and now she's spooked."

"How do you want to handle this?" asked Micah.

"We split apart and hope to hell she has that weapon she stole figured out by now."

When the dock entrance came into view, the two men slowed, brows furrowing in confusion at the sight that greeted them. The deck just past the dock's entrance seemed to be littered with something….

"Are those…?" Jack broke off with a quick glance over at Micah.

"Looks like ball bearings, slathered with a bunch of axle grease," he replied after a moment of study.

Jack groaned. "Of course it is. Damn. Remind me to recruit her ass—just after I *kick* it for placing herself in this kind of danger."

But the expression on the intelligence officer's face told Micah the woman had impressed him.

Jack lifted a fisted hand when they heard a female voice call out from behind a closed door up ahead. He motioned Micah to one side of the door while he stationed himself on the other.

* * *

The control room was a mix of angry secessionists and dismayed Cobalt employees, all frozen in place, anticipating Katie Hyer's response.

Lane had assigned targets, but was holding for Mike's report that Medical was under control before giving the team the weapons-free signal.

Thad waited, rifle painted on his first target. There were eight now, two for each team member. Ell would take out the leader and the one they'd tagged as the most nervous of the bunch. Her third target was Thad's second one, and damn if he wasn't hoping to get there before she did.

He doubted he would; Ell was damn good, the best sniper the Alliance's special forces had.

His target centered firmly in his reticle, Thad accessed the sensor feed Jack had hacked, and found the one for Medical. Pinning it to the team's combat net, he brought it to Lane's attention.

They watched the two SS operatives pass through the entrance and close in on the doctor, weapons raised. The flight surgeon lifted his hands and stepped backward slowly, his words calm, as if he was trying to defuse the situation.

Good luck with that one, Doc.

Mike's voice sounded over the combat net. *{Door to Medical is sealed. I'm right outside.}*

{Why didn't you follow them in?} Ell's tone implied the words '*you idiot,*' but she didn't voice them.

{I may be invisible, hotshot, but drakeskin doesn't mask scent,} Mike retorted. *{You see the sniffer on that dog? He'd know I was there, and he'd out me in a hot minute.}*

{Tell me you have a plan,} Lane cut in.

The demolitions expert sounded offended. *{Of course I do. You have any idea how many volatiles Medical has that I can use to blow shit up?}*

{That's your plan… To blow it up?} Asha deadpanned, her tone stopping just short of incredulity.

{No,} his words dripped with exaggerated patience. *{I'm sending microdrones in to create a spark. Just enough of a spark to make a flash-bang level of distraction. A big boom to shake things up and rattle the enemy. Then I'll rush in and disarm them, see?}*

{Better make it fast,} advised Thad. *{Now that they have the doctor secured, these bastards are trying to flush out our girl. Jack and Micah aren't quite there yet, and we can't have her turning herself in.}*

* * *

The voice from the control center repeated the threat.

*{We know you're out there, Katie Hyer. We have your dog. We have the doctor. Come to the control room, **now**, or we start shooting.}*

"I'm here," a female voice called out.

Micah heard the words both audibly and over comms as it broadcast over the platform's public net.

"Don't hurt them. I'll…I'll come turn myself in."

The ancillary door that led to the mechanics bay flew open, and Micah snapped out a hand, hooking an arm around Katie's waist as she barreled through.

She shrieked and tried to bring her weapon to bear, but Jack disarmed her with one swift move.

"Easy there," said the Marine. "We're on your side. Geminate Navy, Special Forces. See?"

Wild eyes connected first with Micah and then shifted over to Jack, who nodded reassuringly at her while tapping the holopips on his drakeskin collar.

"I'm Lieutenant Campbell, and the man holding you is Lieutenant Case."

"You don't understand, they have my foster dad, and my dog. They'll kill them if I don't—"

"Trust me, we'll get them back for you. We already have an operative working to set them free."

Lane's voice broke in. *{Noble Three, convince that girl to play along. We need to buy Noble Five enough time to secure the doctor before we can make our move.}*

Over Katie's head, Micah met Jack's gaze, and nodded.

{Good copy, Noble One.}

* * *

Seconds later, Thad heard the voice of a young woman come back on over the public net.

"How do I know you won't hurt them if I turn myself in?"

He cocked his head at Lane's silhouette.

The team leader nodded. *{Good job, Noble Three. Keep the conversation going, give Noble Five room to work.}*

Thad could tell Katie's reply had made an impact on those around him. From their expressions, he could see her words had pleased the secessionists, while at the same time deflated the hopes of the Cobalt employees held prisoner.

The SS leader ignored Katie's question. "Come to the central hub with your hands out. No weapons. And don't waste my time; if there's any hint that you might not be doing what you're told, the dog gets it first."

Thad's attention was drawn to movement on the feed from

Medical. As he watched, a bright green speck floated down into the room through the air vent. The marker was generated by his HUD, its green color identifying the stealth microdrone as one of their own, under Mike's control.

Thad watched it float over to a bank of switches and valves inserted into one of the walls next to a diagnostic bed. The green speck was joined by a second one. The two tiny machines hovered there silently for several minutes—doing what, Thad could not tell.

Or maybe not so silently, after all, he corrected as he saw the basset hound's head swivel in that direction.

The pup began to wiggle and squirm in an effort to get free. The secessionist who held the dog cursed, and whacked it upside the head.

Thad saw the animal flinch, but it seemed fixated on the spot where the drones floated.

{Noble Five,} he warned, and Mike responded immediately.

{I see it. No worries, almost done.}

* * *

Back in the mechanics room just off the dock, Katie's eyes had filled with tears, though Micah could tell that she was making a valiant effort to stave them off.

He squeezed her arm, and as she spared him a glance, her spine stiffened, and her chin went up.

"I'm okay," she said.

Jack nodded. "You remember what we said? This is all to buy our man inside Medical the time he needs to disarm the people holding your foster dad—"

"And my dog," she interrupted.

"—and your dog," he amended, "hostage. All you have to do is pretend to play along. Go ahead and answer them."

She nodded jerkily, and sucked in a lungful of air. Squaring her shoulders, she responded to the voice that had ordered her out into the hub.

"Concourse, okay. It'll take me a minute to get there," she said, her tone slightly wobbly, tears evident in her voice. "Please, don't hurt them."

"Good job, Katie. You're doing great." Jack's voice was smooth, his tone pitched to convey reassurance.

He glanced over at Micah and then back to her.

"Now, here's what's going to happen. The suits Lieutenant Case and I are wearing will allow us to disappear from view. You won't see us, but we'll be right here with you every step of the way, Lieutenant Case on one side, me on the other."

She nodded shakily, and Micah bent so that he could make eye contact with her. "Trust us. This is what we do. You going to be okay?"

He saw her lower lip tremble, but then she steadied herself.

"You've got this," he said, giving her an encouraging smile and a light shoulder squeeze. "I'm going to keep my hand right here on your shoulder so you can feel that we're still here with you, but we're going to disappear now, okay?"

She nodded once more.

Jack inclined his head, and then activated his suit. Micah felt Katie jolt as they faded from view, but to her credit, the young woman remained strong.

As one, they stepped out into the concourse and started toward the central hub of the control room.

By Micah's estimation, they'd gone nearly two klicks when he heard a low rumbling noise and felt the deck shiver beneath his feet.

* * *

Those damn green specks were still hovering in place, but at least the dog had subsided. Thad was about to ask Mike for another sitrep when something flickered over the feed.

He could have sworn he saw a tiny spark—and in the next instant, the sensor feed flashed white. A shiver ran through the platform; he felt it through the soles of his feet. It was accompanied by a rumble so low, it was barely audible.

"What was that?" the leader of the secessionists demanded, spinning to face one of his men. He motioned toward the door. "Get out there and see what's going on. Obert, Gardner, report!"

{Ain't going to get anything out of those folks,} Mike's amused voice came over the combat net. *{Subjects neutralized, hostages freed.}*

With Mike's words, Lane exploded into action. *{Campbell, get that girl some cover. Noble team: engage!}*

SIXTEEN

SIERRA TWELVE
MAINTENANCE TUNNELS

IT ALL HAPPENED so quickly, Katie could hardly process it. They were walking toward the control center when she heard a deep, rumbling noise. The floor shuddered beneath her feet, and the next thing she knew, she was being shoved down by an invisible force.

A weight landed on top of her, and she heard a voice shout, "I've got her. Go!"

She recognized the voice as belonging to Lieutenant Case, so the footsteps pounding through the concourse's floor must be the other man's. Katie felt their vibrations through the palms of her hands.

The sound faded unnaturally, though she could still feel the steady thudding beneath her fingertips. She realized with a detached fascination that they must have the ability to suppress sound somehow.

She looked around, her senses on high alert, but the concourse itself remained eerily calm and empty.

"What's going on?" she whispered, fear for Doc and Fred enveloping her as she felt invisible hands urge her toward the relative protection of a nearby column.

"Everything's going to be fine," Case assured her as he pushed her down into a crouch and then covered her body with his own. "Our man in Medical has the last two secessionists in custody. That's what our team in the control center was waiting for. They're engaging now. This'll all be over in—"

He froze, and Katie sucked in a breath, afraid of what his pause might mean.

The next moment, he relaxed, and with a soft chuckle, he lifted his weight off her. "Well, right about now," he finished.

The air in front of her rippled, and the lieutenant came into view.

He reached out and asked, "Need a hand?"

Katie blinked and sat up, disoriented. "That's… it?"

Lieutenant Case nodded, smiling faintly. "That's it."

She remained sitting a moment and studied him. The man was tall and dark-haired with piercing blue eyes, and he stood, waiting patiently, hand extended, as if he knew she needed a bit of time to process.

She finally grasped his hand, and he pulled her effortlessly to her feet.

With a small lift of his chin in the direction of the concourse, he said, "Come on. I'll escort you to Medical. You can see for yourself; the doctor—and your dog—are just fine."

* * *

The next few hours passed in a flurry of activity, and Katie found herself in the center of it all.

First came the dressing-down she knew would come from Doc Slater. The man was angrier than she'd ever seen him. He tore into her with a furious intensity as she sat on the edge of one of the diagnostic beds, Fred cuddled in her lap.

As he paced, he jabbed at her with a finger, his eyes a steely, cold gray. "That was a *fool* stunt you pulled! What in *star's* name made you think you were capable of taking on that many people—*armed* people, might I remind you—all on your own? I taught you better than this!"

This wasn't her foster dad speaking, this was Major Slater of the Geminate Alliance Navy, come out of retirement. She could practically see him reaming out any malefactors under his command.

Shame shafted through her, and she couldn't bring herself to meet his eyes. Instead, she focused intently on the puppy she held in her arms, her free hand playing with one long, floppy ear.

And then she realized: this was all because he cared. His anger was a release valve; it masked the fear he'd felt for her.

Her hand stilled, and she chanced a look up at him.

His voice calmed as he came to a stop in front of her and gripped her by the shoulders. Katie let Fred down onto the diagnostic bed as Doc turned her to face him.

"Katie-girl," he said softly as he gave her a gentle shake. "You're not invincible, for star's sake. You could have been killed. You were in a firefight. You took a life."

Katie flinched. "Are you… mad about that?" Her words were tinged with uncertainty.

He had to be. He was a doctor, committed to saving lives, not taking them. She averted her eyes, unable to face the condemnation she would surely see in his.

Air exploded from Doc's lungs in a great gust. "Hell no, sweetheart… except for the fact that you have to live with it now. That's not an easy burden to bear. It'll take you some time to come to grips with it. I know it did for me."

He gathered her in his arms, his hand tucking her head against his shoulder as he had when she was younger. His voice was muffled, his face buried against the top of her head. "If it comes down to you or them, I'll *always* choose your life over theirs. But just so we're clear, no more scaring me like this, you understand?"

A footfall sounded from behind them, and a throat cleared.

"Katie Hyer?"

Slater released her, stepping back as Katie turned to face the unfamiliar voice.

A woman stood dressed in the same drakeskin suit the two other soldiers had worn. She was whipcord lean, with dark eyes and hair cut military-short, and she exuded an aura of authority.

"Miss Hyer," the woman repeated, and it was no longer a question.

She nodded anyway.

"I'm Captain Lane Reid. If you have a moment, I need to debrief you." She gestured to the hallway outside Medical, her gaze flicking briefly over to Slater's and then back again. "The doctor can join you if you wish. Your call."

Surprisingly, Doc stepped back. The expression he wore was odd, the look in his eyes a mixture of sadness and pride. "You don't need me for this," he said gruffly. "We'll catch up after." He nodded respectfully to the woman, his gaze resting for a brief moment on the insignia on the captain's sleeve.

The woman nodded and walked away.

Without a word, Katie followed. She spied other special forces soldiers along the way, each dressed in the same drakeskin uniform. Everyone she saw seemed either to be conferring with Cobalt security, or hauling gear back to their ship.

They'd even bumped into Lieutenant Case, and he'd given her a small salute and an encouraging nod as he passed by.

She wondered if he knew about the debrief, and guessed he might, given the identity of the woman she followed.

There was just one person seated in the conference room when they arrived.

"Miss Hyer," Lieutenant Campbell greeted as they entered. He gestured to a tray in the center of the table, which held a pair of carafes and some mugs. "Coffee? Water?"

She shook her head.

Captain Reid waved Katie to a nearby seat. "Tell us what happened, please. From the top."

"Well, I guess it started when this ship came out of nowhere and nearly sideswiped *Goblin*," she began, and Jack held up a hand.

"That's the tug you were piloting?" he clarified, and she nodded.

"Continue," the captain said.

With a deep breath, Katie plunged in, sparing no detail—or so she thought. Two hours later, she realized how skillful an interrogator Campbell was; she recalled details she hadn't even known she'd observed.

"And that's it?" he asked when she reached the point in her story where the voice came over the public net and ordered her to turn herself in.

She lifted her shoulder in a half-shrug. "You were there for the rest of it."

The lieutenant sat back, contemplating the mug he held in his hands for a long minute.

After a while, Katie chanced a look the captain's way, surprised the woman would wait so patiently for Campbell to come to whatever conclusion he was mulling over.

He finally straightened, pinning Katie with a look. "What you did today was foolish."

She gulped, and nodded.

"You took huge risks."

She nodded again.

"You killed a man."

She sucked in a harsh breath, swallowed hard, and nodded a third time.

"And you placed yourself—and in the end, your loved ones—in danger."

A little ball of misery began to churn in her gut, and Katie fought the desire to curl into a ball and whimper. She sat perfectly still, muscles locked in a rigid form of attention as her eyes remained glued to his.

Something flashed in their depths, and unaccountably, Katie received the impression that she'd passed some sort of test.

"I… apologize, sir."

Campbell nodded, and a small smile graced his face. "See that it doesn't happen again, Miss Hyer. The Geminate Navy needs people like you. Next time, we might not be around to rescue you."

"Ex–excuse me?" she stuttered, confusion flooding her as she looked from him to Reid and then back.

The captain's face was as inscrutable as ever, but Campbell's had broken into a wide grin.

"Surprised?" He shook his head. "Don't be." He pointed his coffee mug at her in warning. "Not that everything I said wasn't absolutely true, but it's also true that you put a lot of thought into your actions, and you managed to single-handedly neutralize seven of the enemy."

Captain Reid leaned forward, hands clasped on the tabletop. "What the lieutenant means is that the kind of initiative you showed is a trait the Navy looks for in its people. With the proper discipline, we can help mold and shape you, help you reach your best potential."

Katie's mouth opened and closed in wordless protest.

The captain sat back, and then gestured around her. "I'm sure Cobalt Mining is a decent corporation, but have you considered what you intend to do with your life? You have the capacity to be so much more."

Katie looked away. The woman's words struck uncomfortably close to home; they sounded exactly like what Doc had always told her.

"I'll... think about it."

She looked up when a metallic *ting* hit the table. Whatever the object was, Lieutenant Campbell's hand was covering it, but she could hear it scrape as he slid it across to her.

He lifted his hand to reveal what looked like a golden coin. With a small wave, he indicated she should pick it up. "Go on. It's yours."

Katie reached for it, turning the cool metal over in her hands. On one side was engraved the words *'De Opresso Liber.'* On the other was a symbol, a stylized carbyne blade embedded in flame. The same emblem was displayed on the sleeve of his uniform.

She looked up in confusion.

"Hand that to any Navy recruiter, and tell them Team Five sent you."

Beside her, Reid stood. Campbell did the same.

He smiled at her one last time, rapped his knuckles against the top of the table, and said, "Hope to see you again someday, Katie Hyer."

And with that, they were gone.

Later that night, in the privacy of her quarters, Katie hugged Fred close as she sat on her bunk and stared thoughtfully at the coin she held in her palm. Her wire automatically translated the words for her, and something about the phrase, *'To free the oppressed'* struck a chord deep within.

She'd show it to Doc tomorrow, ask him if he knew its significance. For now, she had a lot to process, and Fred was a great listener.

"What do you think, Fred?" she asked softly as she ran a hand down his back. "Ready to be a Navy dog?"

A word from LL Richman

Thank you for reading *Operation Cobalt*. I hope you enjoyed Katie's story. She ends up playing an integral role in *The Chiral Agent*, the first book in the main Biogenesis War series.

If you don't mind, please take a minute to leave a short review on Amazon. Not only would it make this writer a very happy person, but your review also makes a real difference. It's an effective way you can help to keep this series going. The more reviews, the easier it is for new readers to find these tales!

The following pages contain previews from *The Chiral Conspiracy* and *The Chiral Agent*.

Both books are available in print through most booksellers, and in eBook format on Amazon.

Want updates?

Connecting with you as a reader is one of the most rewarding things about writing. I'm active on Facebook at LL Richman's Spacetime Speakeasy. There, you'll receive the latest news about new books, giveaways, get some behind the scenes intel on the science used in the books, plus some really bad dad jokes.

Use the QR code below to get to the Speakeasy, or the following link will take you there: bit.ly/SpacetimeSpeakeasy.

PREVIEW:
THE CHIRAL CONSPIRACY

ONE

PIRATE STATION
STRAITS OF SARGON,
AKKADIA
(ALPHA CENTAURI A)

THE PIRATE STATION smelled like old socks.

Correction, NCIC Special Agent Elodie Cyr thought. *Old socks, worn throughout Hell Walk at the end of Recon.*

She'd become inured to such smells during active duty, first as a Marine, and then later when she joined the Navy's special forces. She'd left the Special Recon Unit four years ago to pursue a career with Navy Criminal Investigation Command, but some things just stuck with you.

Even when you'd rather they not, Ell thought, stifling a sigh.

Her previous life was also responsible for her current situation. She'd been taken hostage with three others, and was now trapped inside an ancient space station with an enviro system that should have been red-tagged before she was born.

The cuffs around her wrists looked like they'd been forged in a prior century, too, but they did the job. The Ziptie nanopackage they'd slapped on her neck before shoving her inside the holding area did the rest. The app blocked the wire in her brain, cutting off all comm and network access.

On the plus side, she could still walk and talk.

The Zipties they'd used back in the Unit were far more robust. They also infiltrated body mods, rendering them inoperable. They also seized control of the SmartCarbyne lattice that reinforced most spacers' bodies, imposing paralysis.

The pirates should have gone for the more comprehensive version, but they hadn't wanted to lug their prisoners' inert bodies around. If Ell had anything to say about it, their laziness was going to cost them.

She had a stash of breach nanobots tucked in the shaft of her left boot, but with her hands behind her back, she'd have to be a contortionist to reach them. Still, it was worth a try.

She shifted, and the guard's attention snapped to her.

"Don't move," he warned.

"Just trying to get more comfortable." She kept her voice even, but continued tucking her legs under her.

"Legs straight, now!" he barked, jabbing the service end of his combat rifle at her, and she froze.

"Okay, okay," she said, extending them back out. "We're good."

The guard frowned at her, but didn't respond. He seemed impossibly young, with a face that looked as if it had never seen stubble.

The hard look in his eyes told her he was well aware of the impression he made, and was determined to overcome what he saw as the stigma of youth.

In the Unit, we would have taught him how to cultivate that misconception and use it to his advantage.

She shook the thought off, resuming her slow perusal of the room. There wasn't much here that could be used to subdue the guard, but that didn't stop her from studying its confines.

Her focus shifted abruptly when she felt a faint nudge against her shoulder. She kept her eyes trained on the baby-faced guard while she let herself lean against her fellow prisoner.

Fingers brushed against her wrist, followed by the sharp scrape of metal as a piece of wire tapped against her palm. Her expression remained unchanged, but she felt a flush of satisfaction as she wrapped her fingers around it.

Well done, Quinn, she thought.

Charles Quinn was still junior enough to be called 'probie,' though Ell didn't. The NCIC office on Hawking was understaffed at the moment, so it was just the two of them, and he didn't need the hazing.

Besides, she'd take one Quinn over three average workers any day. The man was resourceful, and had impressive recall.

This tiny scrap of wire was the perfect example. She'd mentioned her skill with ancient mechanical locks once in passing, but he'd obviously remembered it. Better yet, he looked for a way to take advantage of it.

As she bent the wire into two opposing ninety-degree angles, Quinn worked to distract the guard.

Nodding to the fourth person they'd taken prisoner, he asked, "Don't you think you should check on her? A hostage is no good to you if she's dead."

Ell's fingers traced the upper portion of the lock, gently easing the wire in and applying upward pressure. She felt the ratchet lift.

The guard glared at Quinn. "She's fine. Now shut up."

Holding the wire in place, Ell flexed her hand, pressing against the cuff. She felt the teeth begin to slowly slide through the opening.

"I don't see her breathing," Quinn's voice sounded doubtful. "Couldn't you at least scan her?"

The wire slipped. Ell relaxed her hand on an inhale, wiggling her fingers on the exhale. She tried again. Three more teeth slid through the ratchet and Ell palmed the wire while working her wrist free of the shackles.

"I said," the guard stepped closer, aiming his pulse rifle at Quinn's forehead. "Shut. The. Fuck. Up."

"He'll be quiet," Ell told the guard hastily, then leaned into Quinn, using the movement to reach her hand behind his back. "Stand down."

He nodded and slumped slightly forward, the action a cover to give her better access to his bound wrists.

By the time she had Quinn freed, her shoulders ached. Ell sucked in a slow, deep breath and readied herself to do it all again—this time, to free the man on her right.

Quinn, miming still-bound hands, did what he could to draw attention from her. He cleared his throat. The pirate shot him a narrow-eyed look.

"Our people are coming. When they get here, shit's going down," Quinn said, his tone calm and level. "There's no way you're going to win this."

Before he could continue, the guard scoffed. "What, you think you're someone important? You're just a glorified cop, man."

Quinn's eyes narrowed. "NCIC still goes through basic and advanced, just like everyone else, kid. And then the real training begins."

That's it. Keep distracting him, Ell silently encouraged, as her shoulder made contact with the major seated to her right.

She and Rafe went way back. While she'd been with the Unit, Rafe Zander had flown Shadow Recon. He'd been responsible for hauling Ell's ass out of many a hot zone, back in the day.

Like her, he'd moved on. Unlike her, he'd stayed in the same Navy track. He'd risen to the rank of major, and now commanded an entire squadron.

To her left, Quinn tried a more persuasive tone.

"You know the Navy's looking for us. You have four naval personnel here." He shook his head. "If you let us go now, it'll go easier on you when they get here."

Using her fingers against his forearm, Ell quickly tapped out a code she knew Rafe would understand, one all Unit operators and

Shadow Recon pilots knew. Within seconds, she felt his bound hands brush against hers, and she went to work.

The guard glowered at Quinn, waggling his pulse rifle threateningly. "Who's got the gun and who's trussed up tighter 'n cargo in a net, huh, asshole?"

Quinn walked a tightrope with the guard, alternately persuading and goading.

At times, Ell thought she should mentally rename Baby Face to Red Face. Just when she began to worry Quinn had provoked the guard too far, he backed off, only to begin again a few seconds later.

The technique was the perfect distraction.

Right up to the moment Rafe's shackles hit the ground with a soft *clang.*

What the—?

Ell's stomach plummeted, dismay stabbing through her at Rafe's unexpected clumsiness.

The guard broke off, shooting a suspicious look their way. Motioning to Ell and the major, he ordered, "Move away from each other. Slowly, now."

Ell moved toward Quinn, while Rafe shuffled in the opposite direction. He managed to make more noise with his cuffs, and Ell realized he was doing it to give her an opening.

Ell took it.

Using the man's momentary distraction, she launched her attack. With the flick of a wrist, her handcuffs went slicing through the air, a crude form of nunchaku.

Military-grade picosensors woven throughout her body kicked in as she exploded to her feet, boosting reflexes far beyond the human norm. Quinn and Rafe were right behind her.

Quinn dove for the weapon Ell's handcuffs had sent flying when they wrapped around the guard's wrist. Rafe raced for the downed specialist in the corner.

Ell drove her right shoulder into the guard's abdomen, hand crossing to wrap behind his opposing knee, jerking him off his feet. Instinctively, the guard tried to roll out from under her. She allowed him a half turn before grabbing his arm and forcing it forward.

Snaking one hand under his armpit and the other around his neck, she levered him into a bow and arrow choke hold.

His face already red from exertion, his eyes went wide when he realized his air supply had been cut off. He began to struggle, but then Quinn was there, the guard's rifle aimed unerringly at the man's face.

"Freeze," the investigator barked, and then shrugged with an evil grin. "Or don't. Your call."

Wisely, the young guard froze.

She released her hold about his neck and reached for the Ziptie hidden in the shaft of her boot, while Rafe used their discarded cuffs to bind the guard. She waved the nanopackage at the major before slapping it against the back of their prisoner's neck.

"He had plenty of opportunity to call for reinforcements before I ziptied him," she warned Rafe.

He shook his head. "He didn't." The major jerked his chin at the guard. "Look at his face. It never even occurred to him to call for help."

Ell glanced down at the guard and realized Rafe was right. The guard's face had reddened once more, only this time in embarrassment at the major's words.

The look in his eyes—about the only expressive thing allowed him under the influence of Ell's more comprehensive Ziptie—clearly telegraphed his dismay.

Shaking her head, she gave Baby Face a pat on the cheek, and then rocked back on her heels. Careful not to cross Quinn's line of fire, she rolled to her feet.

Rafe shot her an unreadable look. "You ready to get out of here, Sarge?"

Ell couldn't quite hide her flinch at his use of her old rank, but she covered it by motioning to the fourth prisoner. "Okay, fine. I'll get the door. You grab her."

Rafe lifted a brow. "You forgotten the way we do things in the Navy? Last I recall, majors give sergeants orders, not the other way around."

Ell scowled at him. "I'm not a sergeant any longer," she reminded him. "You're combat; I'm NCIC."

"Ma'am, yes, ma'am," he said, amusement coloring his tone as he stepped toward their prone companion.

Narrowing her eyes, she stood there a moment, studying him. Rafe's actions weren't adding up. She wondered what side game he had going on that he wasn't telling her.

He shot her a knowing look, which told her exactly nothing other than he knew his actions had her mystified.

Ell shook her head, dismissing Rafe and turning to Quinn. She motioned for the door. "You know there is a good chance they have at least one more standing outside. They hear the door opening and they'll have weapons drawn before you can get a bead on them."

Quinn nodded, brows drawing together. "The thought had occurred to me," he admitted. "Got any suggestions?"

"Yeah," she drew the word out thoughtfully, playing out the scene in her mind.

Placing her hand over the door's control mechanism, she deposited a round of breaching nano into it. It synched with the software in her wire, showing her a lock that was easily a decade or more out of use.

"Okay," she murmured. "That'll be easy enough to pick."

She looked over her shoulder at Quinn and then Rafe, who had the fourth hostage hoisted over his shoulder in a fireman's carry.

"Stay clear of the door," she instructed Rafe, waving him over toward Quinn. "Quinn, open the door on my mark. Be prepared to back me up like you did when we took out Baby Face. Got it?"

Quinn nodded and both men stepped back against the bulkhead. Ell moved to the opposite side of the door, crouching low to the deck. "On three. One…two…"

Quinn triggered the door and Ell propelled herself up and into the guard who had turned at the sound. An *oof* sounded from the pirate as he landed on his back, his weapon clattering to the deck.

Peripheral vision told her Quinn had engaged another guard just as the man beneath her rolled. Ell barely escaped the fist that came crashing down toward her face, jerking her head to the left at the last moment.

She thrust her fist upward in what looked like a cross jab. The man's chin jerked back instinctively, but she wasn't going for the chin. Instead, she hooked her fingers around the bony scapula ridge that ran just behind the top of the man's shoulder and *pulled*. That action levered Ell up while propelling the man toward the deck.

The pirate was now face down with Ell on top. She reached for the pistol strapped to the man's right thigh, but the pirate tried to buck her off. Ell fought to put the man in a grappling hold but found herself suddenly airborne.

She landed against the bulkhead with a soft grunt just as she heard the click of a combat rifle and a low, guttural, "Freeze!"

Ell recognized that voice.

She looked up and saw familiar brown eyes, narrowed on the guard she'd been battling. The owner of those eyes gave her a quick look, his smile a brief slash of white against an ebony backdrop, before turning back to glare the pirate.

Thaddaeus Severance was a powerhouse of a Marine, as charismatic as he was strong. Ell had learned long ago she was defenseless against the captain's easy charm, so she wasn't surprised to find herself grinning back at him like an idiot.

The man had won her over the moment they'd first been introduced. Elodie had always hated her first name, had felt it far too flowery for a Marine. His first words had put paid to that.

"El-o-die," he'd rolled the word around in his mouth, his signature smile curving slowly about his lips. "Now that, there, is one badass name."

She'd thought he was hazing her…until he explained.

"Never met someone whose name spelled out what would happen if you messed with her." He'd shaken his head in admiration. "Elo-die. Hello-die. Sweetest combat name I ever heard."

Ell shook off the memory and rolled to her feet as Thad spoke.

The words, though clipped, were spoken in a distinctive and familiar twang as he tilted his head down to indicate his tactical vest. "Zipties, right pocket. Antidote code, left."

She nodded, reaching for the nanopackage.

"Thought you needed rescuing, *ami*," he said in a low rumble only she could hear. "Glad to see my intel was wrong."

"I never say no to a helping hand," she murmured in reply, bending to slap the restraint on the guard Thad had pinned.

Thad gave a low "Oorah," and then snapped his rifle back out to cover the passageway and she crossed to apply the Ziptie to the third guard and hand out antidotes to Rafe and Quinn.

As Ell scooped up the rifle that had gone flying when she first tackled the guard, Thad nudged the pirate. "C'mon *coo-yon*, get up."

Ell shot Thad a quick glance as she helped haul the pirate to his feet. "You alone, Captain?"

"Nope. Jack's with me, as are Asha and Boone."

Ell saw the look that Thad leveled at her when he mentioned those last two names.

Asha, the medic who'd kept her alive after the IED exploded, killing Mike, their teammate.

Boone, the man who had taken her place as the team's sniper, while doctors worked to rebuild her.

She managed to keep her expression neutral, but only just. Moments later, she saw the icon for a combat net pop up on her overlay.

{You're about to have company,} she heard Boone warn Thad as she joined. *{Headed your way.}*

Thad swore. *{How the hell did they know we'd sprung the prisoners?}* he demanded.

{Coincidence, maybe?} Jack's voice sounded doubtful. *{But they're inbound, half a klick aft of your position.}*

A map appeared, showing icons denoting friendlies in green, tangos in red. Five reds were converging on them from three different directions.

{That's no coincidence. Move out,} Thad ordered, gesturing them

to follow. He turned and shot the major a questioning look. "Need help with that hostage, *ami*?"

Rafe shook his head. "I'm good. Lead on, Captain."

Ell fell into a run behind Thad as the big Marine raced toward the hatch and the Shadow Recon ship she knew awaited them. Quinn followed, Rafe bringing up the rear.

Five years, she thought. *It's been five years since I was last with the team. How the hell did I end up back here?*

TWO

WRAITH'S COCKPIT WAS tense and quiet, all four members of her crew focused on keeping the ship's tenuous connection to the pirate station hidden from its residents.

{Asha and I will flank them,} a voice came across the Marine combat net they were monitoring. *{We'll drive 'em to you Boone.}*

{Wait one,} a second voice interrupted, the voice of Boone, the team's sniper. *{Two more approaching. Patrol, coming up rim passageway, spinward side, in five.}*

A two-click acknowledgement followed.

Captain Jonathan Micah Case let the communication flow past him. Anything the Marines needed the ship's crew to know about could come through Yuki, his co-pilot.

Right now, Micah's world had shrunk to a single point, a featherlight connection between the Direct Action Penetrator Helios he commanded and the battered hatch the fast attack craft hovered beside.

The connection between the wire embedded inside his brain and the ship's SyntheticVision system was so deep, Micah couldn't have said where the ship ended and he began.

It was as if the ship wasn't even there. Or, rather, he *was* the ship.

He felt as if he could reach out and touch the accordioned surface of the tube snugged up against the dull silver of the station, though he didn't dare. At the moment, each gesture, even the slightest of hand movements, meant something more. His limbs were the ship's thrusters. Her sensors, his eyes.

Without this deep link, he never could have maintained the delicate balance required to keep an exit point open for the Marines and the hostages they'd been sent in to retrieve. He needed the advantage the SV link provided to remain in perfect sync with the small habitat as it rotated upon its central axis.

Wraith should have been able to lock in a velocity that matched the fusion plant driving the station's central axis, but the plant was old and poorly maintained. Its rate of rotation fluctuated just enough that it required Micah to ride it constantly.

A lesser pilot might find this challenging—but a lesser pilot would not be commanding a DAP Helios. Few could fly an attack craft of *Wraith*'s caliber; fewer still could operate her with such precision.

To a one, those pilots who could lay claim to such a distinction were members of the Alliance's elite Shadow Recon teams.

The sound of weapons fire coming across the combat net indicated the Marines had surprised a small group of pirates guarding the hostages.

{There goes our quiet ride out of here.} Yuki's voice was dry as her hands danced across the co-pilot's console, scanning for enemy spacecraft.

He'd caught the rhythm of the station's lumbering spin. Knowing a smooth patch was ahead, he chanced a quick glance past the station's curved hull to the dense ring of asteroids that lay between them and the gate at the Alpha Centauri system's heliopause.

Micah's mind made the rough calculations as his eyes returned to the umbilical before him. *Three AU and some change.*

His gaze focused briefly on the readout overlaid on his three-hundred-sixty-degree view. The Bravo Charlie that Thad had placed onto the hatch's external access pad still read green. The BC, or breaching canister, was programmed to send false signals back to the pirates' monitoring system to make it seem as if the hatch was still securely sealed.

That was good news. The pirates might know they had intruders, but they couldn't know yet exactly where they'd entered, though all entrances were now suspect. Hopefully, they'd be able to extract before the pirates had a chance to trace their location.

{Three down.} Jack, Thad's second.

{Make that four.} Asha. *{Last one's yours Cap.}*

{Got 'im.} Thad.

On the heels of her comm came Boone again. *{Perimeter's clear.}*

No more words were said, but everyone aboard *Wraith* knew what would be coming next.

It was time to exfil.

The ship's open hatch began to fill with Marines in powered battle armor. Micah monitored both interior and exterior feeds as the first to arrive launched himself through the umbilical.

The man wrapped gauntleted fingers around a handhold, piking himself into the ship with economical movement. In an instant, he had reversed his position, bracing to receive the hostages.

It was then that Will noticed they had company.

{Two technicals just launched,} the flight engineer and crew chief sang out from the cradle behind Micah. Will pushed the feed to him with accompanying data that laid out the specs of each craft.

Both were improvised fighting vessels. One was a small cargo tug with a railgun bolted to its undercarriage; the other was an ancient comm-relay satellite that had been retrofitted with a pair of 5 mm lasers.

The speed at which they shot from the small station's shuttle bay belied their ungainly appearance. Turning in a tight arc, the noses of both crafts aimed for the open hatch.

Inside *Wraith*, the hostages were being pulled inside, one by one, Marines hot on their heels. The first Marine hauled Ell Cyr through the opening and then turned, his hand already extended to catch the next hostage. Ell braced on the other side of the hatch, assisting with the catch and urging the hostage to make a hole for the next person inbound.

Three seconds later, Micah heard a *{Go! Go! Go!}* as Thad sealed the end of the umbilical and pushed it away from the hatch.

{Maneuvering!} was all the warning Micah gave the team. He kicked the nose over, dipping down and away from the two vessels attempting to flank *Wraith* on both sides.

He spared a glance at an internal feed and was relieved to see Thad being hoisted into the ship. Boone reached past him to pull the umbilical in after he cleared the opening. Micah cut the feed when the ship registered full hull integrity, and returned his attention to the aggressors on his tail.

{Incoming,} Will warned, followed by a flash of tracer light that told him the tug's railgun had fired.

The cloud of drones surrounding *Wraith* were under Yuki's control; she'd disengaged their cloaking routine when the technical had showed, flipping them into a point-defense formation.

A pair of them broke off, reconfigured as electronic countermeasures. One of the Dazzlers began to emit decoy EM while the other jammed signals. Yuki engaged the rest of the drones in point-defense, their lasers chewing into the slugs the tug had tossed at them.

{Nina! Steel!} Micah began jinking the ship in an evasive pattern, and his gunner responded instantly. She'd had the two pirate ships centered in the reticle of her RAU-19 triple-barrel railgun ever since Will had identified the tangoes. Now, she went weapons free.

Micah felt the vibration through his deep connection with the ship, heard the small *foomp-foomp* of the railgun as it returned fire. The tug tried to evade but it wasn't built for maneuverability, its makers never envisioning it going head-to-head with a DAP Helios.

The steel rounds slammed into the tug just aft of its tiny cockpit. Though better armored than most tugs, it was no match for the projectiles' closing velocity, and the slugs tore into the small vessel's hide as if it were tissue paper.

The RAU spat another short burst of fire to finish the tug off just as Micah tweaked the ship's thrusters to avoid a laser shot from the converted satellite. Nina reacquired the satellite and took the shot at the same time Yuki unleashed laser fire from point defense to chase down *Wraith*'s wild slugs and incinerate them.

His co-pilot's action was automatic. Once a slug was fired in space, it kept going until it found an object with enough stopping power to arrest its velocity. That might be a non-issue if it ended up impacting an asteroid, but it could just as easily hit an innocent vessel, a mining platform, or a space habitat.

Leaving ballistic ammunition shooting through a populated system was the kind of thing only terrorists and pirates did. Cleanup laser fire went part and parcel with good trigger discipline. If Yuki had been too busy to address it, *Wraith*'s SI would have released a cleanup drone to address the matter.

Tug out of commission, Micah twisted the Helios and Nina let fly a twenty-kilogram tungsten sabot that punctured the center of the satellite and continued through, embedding itself into the pirate station's flank.

Sparks flew from the satellite as its two jury-rigged lasers exploded, the fiery bloom a sharp, attenuated thing, as explosions in a vacuum tended to be.

{Shit! Tacticals were just a diversion, folks.} Will's exclamation was accompanied by the wailing of *Wraith*'s proximity alarms as Micah spotted a salvo of smart missiles appear from behind the station.

He ducked. Connected as he was to *Wraith,* the ship followed suit. The oncoming missiles did as well, their onboard computers compensating for every course adjustment he made.

{Dazzlers,} he called to Yuki. The thought barely had time to form before a full dozen additional drones came shooting out from *Wraith*'s hold.

Had he not known they were there, he might have missed them. Their sensor cross-section was almost indistinguishable until they reached the envelope—and then they lit up, smothering the missiles in a cacophony of EM.

The missiles lost lock on *Wraith*. He saw their noses wobble and dip, seeking the strongest signal that matched the Helios they'd been programmed to strike.

There were too many points in space broadcasting that identical signature; to a one, the missiles turned, locking onto the nearest drone. The impacts were impressive, successive detonations, one after the other, immolating both missile and Dazzler alike.

{Heads up!} Will's voice held a warning. *{Time for the main attraction.}*

The flight engineer's comment was followed by a stream of data detailing weapons load-out as two Akkadian Hydra Mark V fighters, bristling with armament, appeared from behind the curve of the station. *Wraith*'s SI pinged a warning, letting Micah and the rest know the vessel had already acquired a targeting lock.

The SI responded first, sending the ship into a series of complex twists faster than even Micah's augmented pilot's reaction time could match.

He joined in, mixing his own moves with the more predictable computer-generated evasions as laser pulses lanced toward them from the Hydras. He threw *Wraith* into a helical turn, pulling her up abruptly, only to whip her over onto her side in a blindingly fast move.

He did it again and again, corkscrewing through the black in a series of increasingly complex and unpredictable moves, while Yuki and Nina hammered at the attacking vessels.

The Dazzlers weren't as effective when pitted against human-augmented SIs, so Yuki deployed them as auxiliary weapons platforms, harrying the fighters, using their agility and maneuverability to eat away at the enemy's defenses.

Nina managed to sever the fuel feed on one of the Hydra's fusion drives and its accel drop was instantaneous. Micah spared it a look as its pilot veered off at a constant velocity it now had no way of stopping, but that moment of distraction cost him.

The second ship scored a hit on *Wraith*'s flank. The laser bit into the ship's ablative surface, the impacts searing like a hot poker against unprotected skin, before dispersing.

Micah ignored it. He'd long ago grown used to the sympathetic echo of pain that skipped along his neural interface before the SyntheticVision system could dampen it. Quickly enough, it faded, the shot's kinetic and heat energy dispersing through the Helios's picofoam interlayer with minimal effect to the craft.

Twice more, Micah dipped and twisted, thrusters firing in a mad and drunken dance, until one last tungsten salvo ripped through the remaining Hydra's shadow shield, its fusion plant's safety interlocks sending it into automatic shutdown.

"Nice job," he heard, just as a firm hand clapped down on his shoulder and the simulation ceased. The pirate station morphed into a decommissioned destroyer, pulled from a boneyard and towed into place.

The fictional Alpha Centauri gate disappeared off his sensors, to be replaced by a Military Operations Area adjacent to the Hawking habitat, in orbit around Procyon's F-class star, Merki.

The Hydras resolved into a pair of Alliance Novastrike fighters, and the tacticals turned back into standard targeting drones, used for warfare simulations and live-fire test runs when the MOA was active.

Awareness of his physical surroundings inside the ship also returned. As usual, it took a few additional seconds for Micah to extract himself from *Wraith*'s SyntheticVision feed. The sensation felt a bit like surfacing from a deep, crystalline pool.

He shook his head and blinked, eyes refocusing on the man standing between the two pilots' cradles. Rafe Zander grinned down at him, his expression one of mild envy.

"I miss that, you know," he told Micah, his eyes drifting meaningfully to the SV control panel.

Micah quirked a smile, dipping his head in a brief nod of acknowledgement. "Want a rematch? I'll give up the pilot's seat and play hostage this time."

Zander shook his head, a wry twist playing about his lips. "Tempting, but you've traumatized my people enough for one day, Captain. They're a regular Navy squadron, not Shadow Recon, like us." He paused, then corrected, "Like you."

* * *

Ell heard the wistfulness buried in Rafe's tone, and wondered why the man had left Shadow Recon when he so clearly loved it.

We all have our stories, our private reasons.

She heard Thad's derisive snort as he started toward the pilot's cradle.

"All due respect, Major, that's bullshit, and you know it," Thad called out, having clearly heard the exchange. "Once SRU, always SRU, *ami*. The Unit never turns its back on its own."

The Marine had clipped his harness to *Wraith*'s frame just inside the ship's hatch while Micah sent the Helios spinning like a dervish. Exercise complete, he waded past the rest of his team—and those tapped to play hostage like Ell and Quinn—to debrief with Rafe.

The major turned. "Thaddaeus Severance the Third," he intoned, shooting Ell a wink. "Name like that belongs to a rich playboy living it up at the Royal Ganymede, not with some thick-necked jarhead out in space, busting heads together."

Thad grunted, spearing Rafe with a narrow, one-eyed squint. "Don' you be gettin' on my last nerve, there, hoss, or I might just have to forget that a Marine captain doesn't clean a major's clock at poker when we get back to the base tonight."

Anyone could tell the ribbing Rafe was handing out was a running joke between the two. Ell happened to know it dated back to when Rafe captained his own DAP Helios.

He'd inserted SRU Team Five into some of the more dangerous sectors of settled space on more than one occasion. Back then, Thad had been a sergeant, just like Ell.

Rafe had changed jobs. Thad had moved on to captain his own team.

Movement had her looking across the ship to where Boone sat, on the bench opposite hers. His eyes captured hers, darkening as he raised his brows in a silent question: *you okay?*

She smiled and nodded, knowing he saw past the lie. He knew, better than anyone, what she'd given up when she left and he'd taken up her mantle.

Being a sniper for the Unit was more than being a sharpshooter. There were an equal number of missions where the sniper played the role of overwatch, as was the case today.

It was the edge of the spear. It was exhilarating.

It was also where she'd been unable to stop her teammate from triggering an IED that caused explosive decompression, blasting Mike out the jagged hole of a habitat service hatch before she could reach him.

Thad's gauntleted hand had been the only thing that kept her from meeting that same fate. He'd pulled her back, carried her to the ship where Asha triaged her ruined leg, severed above the knee by a jagged metal spar.

Rafe's voice jolted her from her memories. She blinked, breaking eye contact with Boone and letting the reassuring pressure of Quinn's shoulder beside her anchor her to the present.

Looking toward the cockpit, she played back Rafe's last words in her head.

"By the way, how soon do they need you back on Ceriba?" he'd asked the Helios pilot.

She saw Micah shoot Yuki a glance, but his co-pilot just shrugged.

"Got a mission for us, Major?" Micah inquired.

Rafe shook his head. "More like a favor, really. The brass

contacted me this morning, asked if we could route a civilian contractor to a secured location," he explained. "The guy's attending some symposium here in Midland."

Midland was Hawking's second largest city, located in the middle of its four-thousand-kilometer-long span. It was a quick, half-hour shuttle hop away, from Portsmouth to the Midway docking ring.

Micah nodded slowly. "I'd have to clear it with Major Snell back on Humbolt, but I don't see a problem. Where's he need to go?"

"It's on your way. Well, close enough, at any rate," Rafe amended, causing Ell to wonder what secured location he was talking about. "I'll send you the coordinates. It'd save one of my pilots the round trip."

Micah shrugged. "If the major says it's okay, then sure, why not? I suppose the guy's used to military transport, if he's working for the Navy. When do we need to leave?"

Rafe thought a moment. "Sometime tomorrow or the next day should be fine. They've recalled him, but they didn't say anything about it being urgent." He paused. "Of course, that could change. You know how it goes."

Micah grunted but didn't otherwise comment on Rafe's vague response. They all knew how these things worked.

Rafe grinned abruptly, straightening. His gaze swept the ship, encompassing Thad's team and the flight crew.

Slapping a hand on the back of Micah's chair, he added, "Which means…." His eyes lit briefly on Ell, laughter dancing in their depths. "There's plenty of time for the Marines and Shadow Recon to pay up. You guys owe my Navy crew a round of drinks."

"Now, hold on there, *ami*." Thad folded his arms and lowered his head, shooting the major a one-eyed glower.

Rafe's brow rose. "The bet was that you couldn't get in and out undetected." He leveled a finger at the Unit leader. "My people detected you."

Just like that, everything snapped into place with crystal clarity.

"That's because you gave us up to them!" Ell cut in accusingly, shouldering her way forward. "The handcuffs. The fact they knew we'd escaped. You were a ringer!"

Rafe grinned at her, his gaze flipping from Ell, to Micah, and then back to Thad. "All's fair in war, folks. I never said the pirates wouldn't have a plant hanging back with the hostages, now did I?"

Ell saw Micah stifle a grin as Thad stood glowering at the major before shaking his head and stomping aft.

"Damned fuckin' pissant Navy pilots," they heard him mutter, the words a cadence matching his every step.

"Oooh-rah," she heard Rafe murmur under his breath, eyes pinned to Thad's retreating back. "Gotcha."

THREE

Nᴀᴛɪᴏɴᴀʟ Sᴇᴄᴜʀɪᴛʏ Aɢᴇɴᴄʏ
Sᴛ. Cʟᴀɪʀ Tᴏᴡɴsʜɪᴘ, Cᴇʀɪʙᴀ
Mʏʀ (Pʀᴏᴄʏᴏɴ B)
Gᴇᴍɪɴᴀᴛᴇ Aʟʟɪᴀɴᴄᴇ

Tʜᴇ ᴏꜰꜰɪᴄᴇ ᴡᴀs a tastefully understated blend of statesmanship, technology, and high-end security.

Its occupant, the director of the Alliance's National Security Agency, privately thought of it as a gilded cage.

Duncan Cutter's job forced him to spend far more time inside its walls than he cared. It bred a sense of restlessness he found he could rarely shake.

The feeling tended to spike during times of national crisis, when issues that threatened the Geminate Alliance's security came to the forefront.

Like they did today.

A noise alerted Cutter that someone was approaching, but the report open on his holoscreen demanded his attention, and he resolutely kept his eyes glued to the data stream before him.

"Duncan." The word was followed by a quick rap on his open doorframe. Cutter spared a quick look at his AD, waving him in. The assistant director jerked his chin at the open door, a question in his eyes.

Cutter grunted. "Go ahead and close it," he said in a resigned tone, his eyes returning to the report.

Sullivan laughed quietly, triggering the doors shut behind him. "You know it drives your protection detail nuts that you insist on leaving your door open."

"Yet surprisingly, they still manage to do their jobs," was Cutter's dry riposte. He gestured to the display hovering above his desk.

"You read the Vermilion report?" he asked.

Sullivan nodded.

"Sounds a bit dire," Cutter continued, watching carefully for the AD's response.

Sullivan's mouth twisted and he dipped his head in reluctant agreement. "It has the potential to be, or so the science geeks say."

Cutter steepled his fingers and stared thoughtfully at his subordinate. After a moment, he pushed away from his desk and strode to the bank of windows that overlooked the NSA's inner courtyard.

"How concerned are they that this discovery could pose a threat?" he asked.

He heard the rustling of fabric behind him, and knew it for the tell it was. Sullivan had a habit of adjusting the cuffs of his suit jacket when he was nervous.

The man blew out a breath as he stepped up to the window beside Cutter.

"Pretty concerned," Sullivan admitted, "but I can't decide if it's because they aren't sure what Vermilion's ecosystem could do to us, or because they *do* know and it scares the shit out of them."

Cutter barked a humorless laugh. "They're hedging their bets, then."

Sullivan coughed. "You could say that, yes."

The AD waited while Cutter mulled over the implications. By now, Cutter knew his subordinate was used to his manner of working through a problem.

Where some people talked things out and others paced, Duncan tended to go preternaturally still, his entire being focused inward as he turned a problem over in his head, examining it from all angles.

After a good five minutes had passed, Cutter stirred. Inhaling a long, deep breath, he turned and faced Sullivan.

"Have them move the portable gate to Luyten's Star," he instructed. "And notify Admiral Toland that her research station's about to be relocated."

The gate he referred to was a Calabi-Yau Gate, a novel technology recently developed by the Alliance. The Geminate claim that it had transformed interstellar travel was no boast.

The gate's ability to fold the higher dimensions of spacetime, allowing instantaneous travel between one inhabited system and another, had connected distant star nations for the first time in centuries.

The integration of local markets into a true interstellar economic system resulted in a robust growth in trade between the various sovereign systems.

At Cutter's mention of sending deGrasse through one such gate, Sullivan jerked his head back, surprise evident.

"You want to move the station to Luyten's?" he repeated, his tone dubious. "That's an awfully tall order. Are you sure it's warranted yet?"

Cutter looked at Sullivan with mild incredulity.

"It's not as if they haven't done this before," he reminded the man. "They moved it into Sirius's planetary nebula when they were studying the increased output of Big Blue."

"Well, yes, but Duncan—"

"And while they were at it, they developed an entirely new class of mobile magnetic shields for the Helios attack craft," Cutter reminded him, tone sharp.

Sullivan raised a hand in unspoken capitulation.

Suppressing a flare of irritation, Cutter returned to his desk and swept a hand over the holographic unit embedded into it. Minimizing the report he'd been studying, he opened the file that had accompanied it.

A list populated on the screen before them, detailing the Vermilion probe's findings and its potential impact upon the rest of inhabited space.

He turned to Sullivan, one brow lifted. "Did you read the addendum?" he asked.

When the AD shifted uncomfortably, Cutter passed a hand over his face, suddenly weary of this discussion. Dropping his hand to his side, he met Sullivan's eyes, letting the man see his resolve.

"Toland isn't an alarmist," he said firmly. "She says her team is concerned about what that probe sent back from Vermilion. Concerned enough to claim it could pose a clear and present danger to the Alliance. Yes, moving deGrasse is warranted."

Sullivan nodded acquiescence, a resigned look playing about his face.

"It'll take time to spin up an operation of that magnitude," he warned. "Call it...a week to get the gate into place, even longer to move the torus into position to transit. Are we going to use the same cover story we did last time, to conceal deGrasse's existence?"

"Gate down for routine maintenance? Yes. Go ahead and have Leavitt Station post notices." Cutter blanked the holo and sent Sullivan a steady look.

Sullivan straightened and stepped away, taking the hint. "Yes, sir. I'll contact Toland immediately. We'll get it done."

* * *

Admiral Amara Toland's wire implant flashed an incoming message on her heads-up display. She came to a halt when the overlay informed her of the person's identity.

Wheeling, she headed back the way she came, a startled lieutenant jumping out of the way when she exited the officer's mess.

As she strode down the passageway to her office, she instructed her wire implant to accept the transmission.

{Good afternoon, sir,} she began, but the NSA's assistant director brushed aside her greeting, cutting right to the point.

{We're mobilizing deGrasse.} Sullivan's words were blunt. *{You have gate priority. How quickly can you make it to the Procyon heliopause?}*

Toland's lips pressed together at this. It wasn't the decision to mobilize that surprised her. After all, the probe had been a deGrasse project, its findings forwarded from her offices to the NSA.

The swift response, though—that was a bit unexpected.

Then again, she thought with a wry laugh, *Duncan Cutter's never been one to shy away from decisive action before. Why'd I expect anything different now?*

Before answering Sullivan, she pulled up a map of the Procyon system and sent the admiralty's SI a request. She knew the distances in general terms; deGrasse was currently at a secured site in the Atlieka Belt, between the system's two stars, Merki and Myr.

The Belt was a debris disk formed by the remains of Myr's outer core when the star became a white dwarf. The belt had eventually settled into an orbit almost 3 AU from Merki, Myr's F-class sister star.

That put deGrasse a bit more than thirty AUs from the system's heliopause.

{We're a little over an AU from the Hawking habitat right now, and an eighteen-day trek to the gate,} she replied, after scanning through the data the Synthetic Intelligence had sent to her HUD.

She paused the feed when she saw the SI's readiness estimates.

{Looks like we can't push the torus to more than a single gravity, due to some of the more sensitive equipment we have on board right now,} she told him. *{It's going to take some time to lock things down*

and reconfigure for transport, too, so it'll be closer to twenty-one days before we can get there.}

There was silence on the other end as Sullivan digested everything she told him.

{Understood,} he sent with a mental nod. *{Do what you need to do but make the best time you can. We're sending the portable gate through to the other end, so be prepared for a rough ride.}*

Toland winced at that, although she'd known this was coming.

Portable gate transits could get bumpy. Permanent gate installations had regular sweeper ships that cleared the exit points of micrometeorites and other debris.

They had sensors to monitor both ends of every transit point. They enacted temporary blackout periods when shifts in the stellar wind or its interaction with the interstellar medium created local weather events.

The Geminate Navy's utility-class gate enjoyed none of these niceties, and there would be nothing at Luyten's heliopause to cushion their arrival.

Toland's people were used to it, though. The civilian contractors working on deGrasse would just have to suck it up and deal.

{I assume you and Director Cutter reviewed the data files we attached. Do you have any questions for us?} she asked.

{Not at the moment, no,} he responded. *{As you've undoubtedly guessed, the probe has all of us concerned.}*

She sent him a crisp nod. *{We'll follow up on its findings and get this nailed down as quickly as we can, sir.}*

{I know you will, Admiral.}

Sullivan cut the connection as Amara approached her office. The doors slid open and her assistant stood, nodding respectfully.

"Ma'am," he said. "I thought you were headed to the mess for lunch."

Amara grimaced. "That can wait. Please gather the section heads for an emergency meeting in—" she looked at her HUD's chrono, "—an hour. I'll be briefing them on a new assignment at that time."

Her assistant nodded. "You got it, Admiral. Anything else?"

Amara shot a glance in the general direction of the mess hall. "Could you ask chef to drum up something and have a steward deliver it to my office?"

She paused, thinking. "Make that for two. Contact Colonel Fraley and ask him to join me. Looks like we'll be working through lunch today."

An hour later, she and Fraley stood at the head of a conference table in a room just outside the torus's Command and Control center. The dozen faces looking back at her held a mixture of surprise and anticipation at the announcement she'd just made—with one exception.

"We can't leave!" Lee Stinton, their chief scientist, protested. "My lead biochemist is off site at the moment." The man made it sound as if the entire situation was a personal affront to him.

Fraley gave the man a patient smile, one Amara suspected was more than a little forced.

"I'm aware, Doctor," he told the man. "When we realized what the probe had found, I had a feeling this kind of thing might happen, so I contacted Nimitz Base on Hawking and asked them to have a transport on standby, just in case."

Stinton's bushy brows beetled together and he frowned.

"Very well," he said after a moment's thought. "But Peres is scheduled to deliver the keynote at a conference there in two days. He won't be ready to leave until then."

Amara fought to keep her expression neutral in the face of the man's arrogance. She shook her head.

"We need to be underway by then," she said firmly. "I know we're only a day's transit away from the habitat, but that's cutting things a bit too close to our departure window. Please extend my apologies to your man for upsetting his schedule in such a precipitous manner."

She paused and let her gaze sweep the rest of the room.

"We need everyone else back on deGrasse as soon as possible," she said. "Consider all liberties revoked, and personnel recalled."

There were murmurs of acknowledgement all around the table. Toland was relieved to hear Stinton's voice among them.

Though technically a civilian, the chief scientist's contract with the Navy required that he, and all other civilian personnel reporting up to him, adhere to Navy regulations regarding such things.

He tended to conveniently forget that from time to time.

"Very well, then. Please pass any questions or concerns along to Colonel Fraley, and if you run into any issues, know that they'll be dealt with on a priority basis."

Toland pushed away from the table and stood. The room stood with her, those with military ranks saluting. She saluted a dismissal, and then left the room.

Want more of SRU Team Five? Check out **The Chiral Conspiracy** on Amazon, and in Kindle Unlimited.
Use the QR code below, or the following link will take you there: http://bit.ly/C-Conspiracy

PREVIEW:
THE CHIRAL AGENT

DEADLY DISCOVERY

ADVANCED ISOLATION LAB
DEGRASSE RESEARCH TORUS
VERMILION, LUYTEN'S STAR
GEMINATE ALLIANCE

THE SPECIMEN CASE was unique. Tucked away in deGrasse's Advanced Isolation Lab, it was disguised as a large gray shipping crate, purposely mislabeled as cleaning supplies. One look inside instantly dispelled that fiction.

It contained no solvents, no soaps. Yet neither was it a standard specimen case. There were no compartments designed to isolate biological samples, laid out in neat, sterile rows.

Instead, opening this case was like falling into a looking-glass microcosm teeming with native life. Segmented into four terrarium-like vivariums, each biosphere was host to its own species: insect, arachnid, rodent, reptile.

The specimen case was unique in another significant way. The biospheres within were engineered from unique molecular building blocks found on Vermilion, the sole habitable planet orbiting Luyten's Star. The life found here was unlike anything else humankind had discovered in all their centuries-long exploration of the universe.

For all but a select few in the Geminate Alliance, it didn't exist.

When the first reports made their way to Alliance headquarters in Procyon, the decision was made to place Luyten's Star under interdiction. The discovery was deemed too dangerous, too easily weaponized. Until Geminate scientists could fully decode what they'd found, all information pertaining to the discovery had been classified, reports redacted.

The Navy's premier research station was secretly relocated to Luyten's Star, and placed in orbit above Vermilion. DeGrasse was staffed by a small team of civilian researchers under contract to the Alliance. These were recruited by the Navy's Advanced Research Agency, and sworn to secrecy about their work.

The decision to interdict Luyten's Star had been made in the hope that news of the discovery could be contained, the sensitive information hidden from the prying eyes of Alliance enemies.

They failed.

AWAKENED

LOCATION: UNKNOWN

"HOLY—! SARGE... IT's alive!"

The exclamation pierced through the fog that cocooned Micah's mind. Distantly, it registered that he was lying on his back, somewhere cool and dark. With effort, Micah pushed against the mental haze that clung to him like a sticky web. His limbs felt leaden, his eyes refused to open.

A second voice joined the first.

"Of course it's alive," the sergeant responded. "It's biomatter. Living tissues and shit."

The sergeant's gruff tone reminded Micah of his drill instructor back at OCS—the kind of person who didn't suffer fools or idiot officer candidates.

The sergeant wasn't done. "Just do what the eggheads in research ordered and burn it." He barked the order, his voice growing louder as he neared Micah's location. "Or do I need to shove my boot up your ass to get you to do your job?"

"But I have neural activity on scan," the first man protested.

"That's a *person* in there, Sarge, not biomatter. Already sent a ping to let Doc Janus know." Agitation was replaced by urgency as his voice drew near. "Hey, grab the emergency kit by the door, will ya? I've got to get him out of there."

Micah heard the sergeant sigh. "Dammit, corpsman. Why'd you have to go and run a scan?" His tone was a mixture of annoyance and exhaustion. "Couldn't you have just done as Janus ordered? Now *I* gotta do as he ordered."

Those words stirred a vague sense of unease in Micah. It turned to alarm when he heard the sound of a firearm being unholstered.

He fought to throw off the haze that clouded his mind, to reach out, call a warning.

"Sarge? What… wait—"

The corpsman's words cut off at the sound of a directed energy weapon being discharged.

Micah's gut clenched; he knew what that meant.

"Sorry about that," the sergeant muttered. Footfalls closed the distance as he stopped in front of the dead corpsman. "You were a good kid, too."

There was a grunt, followed by a soft scraping noise, and annoyance returned to the sergeant's voice.

"Well, hell. Now I have two bodies to dispose of. You damn well better be good for the credits, Janus," the man muttered, "or I might have to pay your pogue ass a visit."

Janus. Micah forced his mind to latch onto the name. Not that he was in any position to share the information at the moment.

In a moment of clarity, he recalled the evanescent wave nanocircuitry wired into his neural net. It was something every Alliance citizen received when they came of age, but Micah's wire had been upgraded when he joined the Geminate Navy. The implant was military-grade and encrypted, allowing him to connect to any secured network.

He reached mentally for it, cursing his drug-induced fog. His thoughts were clumsy, his implant a slippery and elusive thing.

A thundering scrape of metal above his head interrupted his

attempt to connect with the dormant unit. His brain nudged at him, the sound vaguely familiar. Something landed with a dull thump overhead.

The corpsman's body.

A spike of adrenaline cleared his thoughts, and he realized what his subconscious mind had been trying to tell him. He knew now where he was being held: inside an incinerator.

His limbs twitched as he strained to overthrow his paralysis. He had to get out before the thing fired up.

Easy there. You'll be fine.

The thought startled him, seeming to come from nowhere, but he'd run out of time to analyze.

With a deafening roar, the incinerator fired up. All around him, the inferno raged, heat building in the darkness until he knew no more.

* * *

"Shit. He's not dead."

Micah jolted back to awareness as the words brought memory flooding back. He was still supine, still in complete darkness. He was as surprised to find himself alive as the voice sounded.

From what he could tell, his situation hadn't changed, although he seemed to have a clearer head this time around. He had no idea how long he'd been out, but he remained unable to move, to speak, or even to open his eyes.

The voice sounded again. It was the sergeant from before.

"Now what do we do? Janus said we need to scuttle all the evidence before fifteen hundred hours."

His query was met with a curt response.

"Then kill him again, soldier. And this time, check your work."

The new voice was female, her words chilling. They galvanized Micah; he fought for mobility, to no avail.

The sound of soft footsteps heralded her departure, followed by the sergeant's softly muttered, "Damn Akkadian. I didn't sign up for this shit."

The man began to move toward Micah's location, but was brought up short when a resounding *clang* sounded in the distance. The noise elicited a string of curses from the man, the words fading as he ran to investigate.

In the next instant, Micah felt a slight breeze caress his skin. Within seconds, his mind was much more alert than it had been mere minutes before, when he'd clawed his way to consciousness. His arm bumped against a smooth surface, and he froze, arrested by the knowledge that he could now move.

This was a significant improvement.

He turned his attention to his surroundings, to finding a way out of his confinement. The cushion of chilled air around his face suggested close quarters. He reached a cautious hand up and met resistance, ten centimeters above him. The coldness leaching from the material into his palm suggested some type of metal.

He pressed his other hand beside the first, then slid both apart, using the movement to measure the space that held him. Another twenty centimeters, and both hands stopped, having found the sides of his prison.

It suddenly registered that *he* was cold.

Where the hell am I?

There was the briefest of pauses, and then an answer sounded inside his head.

Base Morgue. Level -10. DeGrasse Torus. Luyten's Star.

The words jolted him. These weren't his thoughts. He knew this with certainty, but *how* he knew escaped him, since they hadn't come across his wire. After almost two decades living with the unit embedded in his skull, he'd become used to feeling the presence of the neural implant. It was always there in the back of his mind, like subliminal white noise.

Until now. Its silence was glaring, and yet a voice was unmistakably there.

Deal with it later, Case, he told himself. *Survival first.*

He ran his hands blindly along the seam of his prison walls, seeking a way out. His fingers stilled momentarily as it came to him that his wire wasn't his only nonfunctioning implant. His optical augments weren't working properly, either.

He should have been able to scan the area on all EM bands, the coolness of the metal above him registering in muted blues and purples. Instead, he was enveloped in an unrelenting blackness.

Now would be a good time to leave.

With this newly transmitted thought came movement. The darkness split above his head, broken by a shaft of light. His eyes slitted shut in response to the sudden brightness. The light played down his torso as the platform on which he lay slid out of the wall— a wall of identical drawers, each the exact dimension of the space that confined him.

And then it hit him. He wasn't just in the base's morgue, as the voice had indicated. He was on a freaking *slab* in the morgue, in one of its self-contained storage units, each of which could be individually incinerated.

Which explains why I'm still alive, he realized. *Somehow, my unit must have malfunctioned.*

He turned his head, eyes darting about the room. He was alone, the sergeant nowhere to be seen.

Expelling a breath, Micah sat up. The chill air hit his naked flesh as he assessed his condition.

Get dressed.

The mental words were punctuated by the sound of a locker opening against the far wall. Micah gripped the side of the platform, the sharpness of its metal edge grounding him as he considered what to do.

Shaking his head, he hopped down from the cold, steel surface. As he strode toward the locker that sat invitingly open, thanks to his mysterious benefactor, he reviewed what he could recall of deGrasse.

He knew the morgue was on the military side of the torus. He'd been here once before, to....

His mind hit a blank wall.

Frustrated, he grabbed the boots that sat atop a folded flight suit, dropping them to the deck beside his bare feet. He reached for the clothing but stilled, his fingers already wrapped around the fabric, when he saw the weapons the suit had hidden. A pulsed energy sidearm lay beside a sheathed tanto knife. The first was a civilized, non-lethal weapon; the second was a brute-force instrument.

He knew the tanto's carbyne-edged blade would have twice the tensile strength of graphene and, though he'd never had occasion to test it, could likely cut into bulkhead. One glance at the maker's hallmark stamped into the handle also told him the knife would be perfectly balanced. It wasn't the kind of weapon one wielded against one's fellow soldiers.

Micah's eyes narrowed thoughtfully as he contemplated the unlikely duo.

An unspoken mental nudge spurred him back into movement.

Shrugging into the suit, he grabbed the sidearm, clipping it and its spare batteries onto his belt. He left the tanto for now, as he shoved his feet into the boots, tucking his pantlegs into the tops and sealing them.

He stood—then froze, attention arrested by his reflection in a nearby mirror. The flight suit was standard-issue. Unremarkable, except for its missing rank and nametag. But his face... it looked wrong, somehow.

He raised a hand, running it through short-cropped hair in confusion, stiffening as realization struck.

Micah was left-handed, and yet he'd reached with his right. His hair, which stubbornly grew in one direction, now fell to the wrong side. He leaned closer, noting other subtle irregularities in the face that had stared back at him for the past thirty-five years.

What the—?

They're coming. Leave now if you want to live.

The words were followed by a panel sliding open in a nearby bulkhead. Across the room, Micah heard the pounding of feet in the passageway leading to the morgue. The sergeant was returning, and he wasn't alone.

Leave. **Now**.

There was a sense of urgency to the words that propelled him forward.

He spun and lunged for the tanto blade. Palming it, he slammed the locker door closed and turned to face the yawning blackness.

"Who the hell are you?" he demanded, slipping though the panel.

It slid shut behind him, darkness enveloping him once more.

An image appeared in his head, a mental construct of a lab he knew he'd never seen and yet somehow recognized. The feeling of familiarity wasn't coming from him. It emanated from the same place as the foreign thoughts that he now understood were being pushed to him from… someone else.

Your destination. Hurry.

"Who *are* you?" he repeated as he followed the mental nudge that urged him forward.

There was a pause. The response, when it came, had him reaching for the bulkhead to support himself, his mind spinning in confusion.

I am you.

The Chiral Agent can be ordered from most retail book outlets.

Don't Miss a Thing!

Connecting with you as a reader is one of the most rewarding things about writing. I'm active on Facebook at LL Richman's Spacetime Speakeasy. There, you'll receive the latest news about new books, giveaways, get some behind the scenes intel on the science used in the books, plus some really bad dad jokes.

Use the QR code below to get to the Speakeasy, or the following link will take you there: bit.ly/SpacetimeSpeakeasy.

TERMINOLOGY

Helios – Fast-action spacecraft, considered the workhorses of the Alliance Navy, and capable of carrying an entire squad of fully-kitted Marines. A small percentage of Helios are modified as a Direct Action Penetrator stealth unit.

All DAP Helios vessels are assigned to the Geminate Alliance's Special Reconnaissance Unit, often referred to as SRU, or simply, The Unit.

The teams that fly the DAPs are known as Shadow Recon. They deploy on classified missions, inserting elite special operations teams into destinations where conventional warfare is inadvisable.

DUET Wires (aka "the wire") – DUET stands for Direct Uplink Evanescent Telecom. Much to the dismay of the corporation that invented the tech, that name never took hold. Commonly known simply as 'the wire,' a DUET implant is embedded within every human when they come of age, and is included as a part of the educational system of most sovereign star nations.

Receiving a wire must wait until the brain has reached certain development criteria, as its integration evolves after the initial implant.

Calabi-Yau Gate – This method of folding space bends the compactified branes stacked within the bulk of hyperspace, allowing for instantaneous travel in normal spacetime, from one location to another, regardless of distance.

Scharnhorst Drive – The Scharnhorst is an interstellar drive that generates a Casimir bubble. This allows the drive to harness the Scharnhorst effect, a phenomenon in which light travels faster than c. The drive allows a ship inside its bubble to travel at triple the speed of light.

SmartCarbyne Nanofloss – Carbyne, a chain of single carbon atoms, has twice the tensile strength of graphene. A lattice of ultrafine carbyne filaments, when implanted, will reinforce bone, muscle, and sinew.

Some branches of the Geminate Navy receive a variant of carbyne nanofloss, which functions as an endoskeleton implant.

SmartCarbyne is a unique variant, capable of altering its state. It was originally created to protect military pilots during high-g maneuvers. Its ability to turn 'on' and 'off' made it ideal for protecting the soft tissues of vital organs.

A SmartCarbyne lattice is controlled by an implanted accelerometer. When disengaged, the atoms are in a disorganized, soft state. When experiencing acceleration greater than what the human body can withstand, the lattice automatically hardens, protecting the pilot.

Spike – Special operations electronic breadcrumb trail, only useful at short range. Each spike has a unique geometric signature. That signature is contained in the Alliance military database. An app registers the negative space created by each spike on whatever surface it resides. Once a person or item has been spiked, the search app keeps track of the void that particular spike makes, pinpointing its location while it remains in range.

TENGs and PENGs– Triboelectric nanogenerator batteries are power-harvesting batteries that capture the electric current generated through contact of two materials, converting movement to stored energy. PENGs are piezoelectric nanogenerators that charge using ambient sound in the atmosphere around them.

Ziptie – The ziptie is a nano breach application used as a restraint. Once placed onto exposed flesh, the app immediately unpacks itself, blocking an individual's wire from transmitting a call for help, and rendering body augmentation inert. A military version can take control of a soldier's SmartCarbyne endoskeleton, rendering the victim temporarily immobile.

WEAPONRY & ARMOR

Dazzlers – Decoy ECM (electronics counter-measures) drones, usually under the command of a flight crew's co-pilot. Each drone emits ECM and can jam signals, robbing enemy ships of their ability to coordinate their attack.

Banshees – Fighter-bomber drones, usually under the command of a flight crew's co-pilot. Each Banshee mounts a five-centimeter laser, and is capable of strafing runs. In addition, each carries a pair of missiles, their yields varying by Banshee model type.

Griffins – Stealth drones encased in highly covert layers of high-performance electromagnetic shielding that hides the EM signature of small but powerful fusion reactors so efficiently, the cross-sectional return disappears within a star system's heliospheric current sheet.

CUSP – Compact Ultra-Short Pulse pistol uses a pulsed, laser-induced plasma to either paralyze, flash-bang, flash-blind, or deliver searing pain, depending on the weapon's setting.

P-SCAR – Pulsed Special Combat Assault Rifle.

RAU-19 – Railgun mounted on DAP Helios attack craft.

ALSO BY LL RICHMAN

The Biogenesis War Series
The Chiral Agent
The Chiral Protocol
Chiral Justice

The Biogenesis War Files: The Early Years
Operation Cobalt
Ambush in the Sargon Straits
The Chiral Conspiracy
Sudden Death

The Vision Rising Series
Vision Rising
Vision's Gambit
Vision's Pawn

The Battlefield Diplomacy Series
Battlefield Diplomacy
Lost Colony
Insurrection

The Enfield Genesis Series
Alpha Centauri
Proxima Centauri
Tau Ceti
Epsilon Eridani
Sirius

The Sol Dissolution Series
Venusian Uprising
Assault on Sedna
The Hyperion War
The Fall of Terra

ABOUT THE AUTHOR

L.L. Richman has a diverse career background, having spent more than a decade working in radiation physics, and twice that as a director of film and video. An avid pilot and photographer, Richman can often be found flying a Piper Cherokee or photographing Deep Sky Objects (DSOs) late at night.